VIA Folios 176

Coquina Soup

Published by Bordighera Press, an imprint of the John D. Calandra Italian American Institute of Queens College, The City University of New York.

25 West 43rd Street, 17th Floor, New York, NY 10036

Library of Congress Control Number: 2025931118

Cover art and design by Mishou Sanchez.

© 2025, Frances Nevill

VIA Folios 176
ISBN 978-1-59954-217-1

COQUINA SOUP

Collected Stories

FRANCES NEVILL

BORDIGHERA PRESS

For My Daughters

*Keep your faith, your sunny outlook, and always make time
to collect seashells along the beach.*

TABLE OF CONTENTS

BREAD OF THE MIZER

I am riding in the car with my soon–to-be ex-husband as he takes me to the hospital to see my mother.

He tries to engage me. "Do you think they're feeding her well?"

I want to have an answer to this question. I want to care about what they're feeding my mother who has dropped to ninety pounds and who took things too far as her boyfriend called the police, triggering the law to step in and take her to some run down facility. A few phone calls from my husband's lawyer friends and we finagled her into a fancier place touted as smelling more like lemons than piss.

I want to think about the quality of the food they feed my mother, but instead I'm thinking about the paint swatches I saw on my husband's kitchen counter in the condo he's rented during our separation. Four shades of grey, spread out like a poker hand by his girlfriend, Flaire. Flaire, (if that is even her real name) the interior decorator who my friend said could help me order window treatments to block the blaring sunlight. Flaire, who fucked my husband while I was at night school working to get my certification to become a paralegal. Flaire, who is now selecting finishes for the love nest my husband is rumored to be buying with her, but never had the money to build with me.

"I don't know," I finally answer and wonder if they selected the grey that looks like cigarette ashes on a bar floor or the darker grey that looks like pigeon feathers on a sidewalk. I hope they choose the pigeons. I hope it's a pending decision. I hope their life isn't moving forward and that they're suspended in time.

An hour passes as I work on my laptop in the passenger seat, writing a paper that's due. Kevin's focus shifts from the road to his phone; the road to his phone. Back and forth. I wonder if he is looking for a text from Flaire. I try to appear focused on my paper, and the sound of me pecking the computer keys fills the void.

I wonder why I let him drive me. Why I feel I need the support. Would seeing my mother in this place cause me to skid off into some lonely, hellish place? Had I become this helpless? A piece of me still wants him to want me. A piece of me is admiring him in the periphery of my vision. The late afternoon sun casts a shadow across his face highlighting his tan skin. He is handsome. A piece of me still thinks maybe I have a chance. Maybe he'll see my mom in this place and feel a care and concern for me and want to stay. For the moment, I go with this. I hang onto this.

"Hope she's at least sleeping well." He tosses this in as if scripted. I have a little hope inside me that's thinking his concern is real. I want that small part of me to stay open to this idea. If it's true and if there is a future for us, I want to keep the pathway clear.

I reach for some mints he keeps in the center console and let my hand brush against his resting forearm. Maybe in this small exchange he might feel a warmth between us—a connection. Instead, he flinches and his forearm moves not more than an inch, yet it feels like endless space that I cannot corral.

I watch the clock on my laptop counting down the minutes until we finally arrive at the front entrance of the hospital, if one can call it that. I'm still not clear if the intention of this place is to help her or fool her. The exterior is a surprise. I expect to see tall sterile buildings reminiscent of the days of sweatshops, child labor and tuberculosis sanitariums. Instead, a round fountain sprays water upward like fireworks and a row of sable palms line the half circle entrance. Looking closer, I see this is not any fountain. It is opaque and lifelike. It rumbles and looks three-dimensional like a fountain, but it is in fact, a hologram. It is massive and greets you like a beacon. A feeling of safety washes over me. A place this pretty can't be scary. A place like this has to be safe.

"Looks like a resort." Kevin cuts the wheel a sharp left so he can back into a parking spot. One habit, I tell myself, that I no longer have to endure if we divorce. I hate how he always has to back into parking spots and then turn the wheels at a sharp angle like the goddamn car is posing for paparazzi.

He comes around and opens my door and is in awe of the fountain. "I read about this place," he says. "They got a huge donation from the family of a patient who killed himself. A tech prodigy."

I remember the story, too. He was a college kid who came up with something that advanced the use of holograms. The family wanted his work to be used as art for the patients. I watch the fake bubbling overflow of water spilling into the base of the fountain that forms a pool deep enough to swim—or drown—in.

He takes my hand to help me out of the car.

"Let me say again that I'm glad you let me come. Our relationship might be changing, but Jean will always be family."

I notice a pile of dog shit in the grass as I let his words find a place to land. We walk toward the entrance. I have been warned by my attorney to be wary of these pleasantries. Kevin is worried about what I will ask for in the divorce. He's trying to advance things quickly with Flaire. They are in love and there's nothing I can do about it. Flaire comes with a price I never did. She is tall, with red locks that bounce when she walks. She is from Ireland. And she is expensive. She is a decorator and she likes all the extras that most people cannot afford. Kevin will have to pay a price for her that I didn't cost. I made myself virtually free of charge. I made a mistake by helping him through law school. The girlfriend is never the wife, so the saying goes about law school or medical school lovers. I thought I had this beat since we married prior to him starting school. First, we'd get him through law school and then my turn would come. It wasn't that easy. Law school took its toll on the both of us. I worked more hours than I should have so he didn't have to take out huge loans. And then, the first few years of him establishing himself in the legal world seemed to never come with any downtime. With my resolve lost, I am now struggling to finish paralegal courses.

He lets go of my hand and we reach the entrance of the hospital. I hope that he will reach for it again in a gesture made of something other than politeness. He doesn't. I think about reaching for his, but I am already embarrassed by the rejection I know I'll get. As we walk through the doors he and I cross the threshold like a couple. I think, in some twisted logic, that maybe this can be a new beginning. Whatever it is that we are doing together in this moment, it is ours alone: no Flaire. I can have him in this space, for this moment, and he is mine.

There's another hologram fountain inside. It is smaller and dripping with the sounds of chimes as water hits a shallow pool with a wide edge around it. The floor of the fountain is covered in pennies. Instinctively, I reach inside my purse, searching the bottom to find a few coins, before realizing even the pennies are fake. I can see the outlines of thousands of Abraham Lincolns in brown. The water is cloudless and ripples across Lincoln's many faces, and I want to reach my hand in and scoop them up. I feel Kevin tap his hand on my shoulder.

"Kevin and Mandy Markum," he tells the ginger-haired receptionist. She is pretty and her glassy eyes change color with shifting light. I think of Flaire and her auburn waves that have gradient changes in hue like desert sands. I wonder if Flaire is a true redhead. It bothers me that Kevin knows the answer.

"We're here to see Jean Myers," he says. My mother continues to keep this name even though she hasn't been a Myers for decades, since I was a small girl. She is a Dunkle by birth. Dunkles are poor—so poor they're not considered anything at all—not poor white trash, not low class. It's like they aren't even there. Growing up, I often wondered where Dunkles came from and why I was born into them. Dunkle boys cause fights in bars, run drugs, and beat women. Dunkle girls start fights in bathrooms, work three jobs, and are perpetually pregnant. Myers was a step up for my mom, but not by much. Travis Myers was reliably unemployed and abusive—a dry drunk. Travis Myers is—was—my father. Now, he's six feet beneath rural Florida red clay and every time a hard rain comes through I hope whatever it is that he was made of doesn't seep into the aquifer.

Kevin and I are led down a long hallway. It's open visitation hours at this hospital yet there are few people visiting or socializing. Patients are seated at tables and are quiet, obedient. It feels like we've come to an old-folks home. No one here seems violent or on crack or on the verge of tossing a bomb into a building or doing what Jean did that night. But looking closely, I spot health care aides at every doorway and some seated at the tables alongside the patients. They blend in and look like they could be patients themselves. Only small nametags give away their identity.

Kevin's cell phone vibrates and a startled health care aide quickly motions to him.

"Sir, you'll have to take that back out to your car."

Kevin apologizes. I realize I have my purse and remember I'm not supposed to. He takes my purse and I wait while he runs back out of the facility to return these things to the car. I notice him putting his phone to his ear as he exits through the double doors. She's calling him. I know.

When he returns we take a seat in a small waiting area on a worn navy leather couch that we sink into, forcing our shoulders to touch. Kevin reaches for my hand. "I'm here if you need me." I squeeze his hand. He doesn't squeeze back. His hand is limp, but I still hold it. Someone in a smock comes by and asks us if we'd like some water. I look at Kevin to see if he wants any.

"Sure," he says. The smocked girl points him to a table where they've put out some bottled waters for visitors. My mom asked that I bring her make-up, but the staff told me earlier that nothing from the outside can come into the hospital.

Kevin hands me a bottled water. I say no thanks out of some spinning logic I have that by not drinking the water will mean more for him later.

Kevin paces a bit looking through double doors that overlook a courtyard. People stand around what looks like another fountain.

"Jean!" I hear Kevin and turn as he reaches out for my mother. He hugs her and I cannot see her face or her body. Her hands are on his shoulders, the ends of her grey bob brushing against him.

And then he backs away. My mother comes into view. It has been thirty days since the incident that brought her here. She looks like a baby. Her cheeks are full, no longer the sunken gaunt face I remember in the weeks that led to the night her long-term boyfriend threw her out of their house. His house, technically. She was always just a guest, but over time she grew to forget that fact. Not me. I didn't forget and I lived in worry for her safety. I knew he hit her. I knew he called her the worst names. I knew he binged on the cheapest, foulest liquor. He smoked unfiltered cigarettes that stained his teeth, the smoke creeping its way into my mother's aura. After decades together, the pores in her skin resembled scattered coffee grounds on a white countertop. Her prettiness poisoned with his habits and ways. A steady diet of mizer's bread.

Sadly, I also knew that anything unique in her never really had a chance to take root. Her Dunkle start in life came with a seed of submission that was planted in all the Dunkle women. To remove it would take digging up roots buried so deep you'd never find their origin. You'd think you'd uprooted it, only to find more wispy remnants. You'd turn your back and like weeds growing in the drippy, dog-day heat, they'd spread when you weren't looking. Those weeds overtook my mother.

Her eyes now look like what I remembered they looked like when I was a child—they had a glisten to them that attracted attention from men and a sparkle that seemed to communicate laughter, and a good time, despite her origins. She didn't have that zombie look of a medicated psych patient that you see in the movies.

I walk toward her.

"Mandy." She hugs me.

"You look great, Mama." I say the words but struggle to see all of her face. I see reflections that look like who I knew when I was a child, and it is those ripples of memory like broken pieces of mirror on a floor that always have me disoriented in her presence. I am not sure what image I should look at and the confusion of my own image projects off the broken glass and into my sight line. In her presence, this vertigo never seems to pass.

She nods. She looks at me as if to decide how I will be handled, played. Am I daughter? Or friend? I look over at Kevin and he motions toward the door. "You two go visit."

"Why don't we go outside, Mama?" I take her hand and we walk through the double doors leaving Kevin to drift off into thoughts I know involve Flaire.

Mom doesn't know Kevin and I are separated. I'd tried telling her weeks and weeks ago, before the incident, but I couldn't speak it. I had hoped she might sense it and help pull out the truth.

We sit on a concrete bench that overlooks a winding koi pond that has a dark bottom like what I imagine a hidden lagoon looks like. Red and black koi dart through the water that billows as they pass. The koi pond is also a hologram. The fish are robust and fleshy and are the most lifelike of all the holograms I've seen so far.

"Have you had much luck this month?"

I know what she is talking about. I wish she hadn't brought it up.

"No." I watch the koi. They've changed color in the few seconds since I turned my gaze. They're now orange and green. They are like swirling marbles in a tide pool and they dart and chase each other. They disappear and reappear like giddy children on a playground playing hide-and-go-seek. I am enchanted for a moment and I reach toward the koi, fascinated by their colors swirling around in the water. I place my hand along the top of the water that looks iridescent and reflects light like a prism. I see a koi coming toward me and a twinge of anticipation comes over me as I hope I'll get to brush up against it. I feel nothing. Just air.

"I'm sorry," she says, looking at the fish, her hands folded on her lap.

I want to touch my stomach and feel a sense of life, but I don't. It's become one of many empty places I can count inside me.

I want to talk to her more about it. I want to ask her if it will ever happen. I want to tell her Kevin is moving on to a woman who can fill spaces in houses and spaces in her body with things I cannot. But my mom looks right through me as if she's spotted what she was looking for.

"Have you seen Buoy?"

Mom, really? But I knew it was coming. I knew that is why I am here. I knew this is the reason she probably looked forward to the whole day.

I didn't know how to tell her that Buoy Mize is the reason she is here.

"Nah," I say. "Mom, I won't be seeing Buoy."

Buoy has a restraining order against her, though he's the abuser. Another way he twisted the truth to the law. He tossed her things in a dumpster after that night. Then he called me, in a rare moment of remorse, I figured, to ask if I wanted a drawer full of family photos, including my baby album. When I went out to the property, I couldn't find him. He'd left me a note saying my things were in the detached garage. When I walked into the old pine-board structure, there were a few fruit boxes that were soft from water damage. In one of them, I found a shoebox filled with photos from childhood and a photo album of me and my sister, Misty. Misty lives out of state now because she couldn't bear living anywhere near our little town of Pikes. She couldn't bear being close to Mom and Buoy and the life they were living. She feared being "infected" by our mother's submissive ways and moved and moved until she was too far away to know us anymore.

The book and album showed signs of water damage, too. I carried the box to my car and knocked again on the door, but Buoy didn't answer. I knew he was hiding from my knocking. I knew that if he had to look me in the eye, he'd see my mother. And he marked the end of that chapter the night she did what she did. I couldn't get a good view inside but he was sitting as he always did: in a recliner spitting tobacco into a plastic cup that had lost its color from years of my mother putting it through a hot cycle, trying to keep things clean for him.

"Will you see him this week?"

"Why would I want to see him, Mom?"

"He always liked you, Mandy." And this is where she starts trying to campaign for my forgiveness of him. She's starting to build a case for their reconciliation. She thinks that her old prettiness will trump the current ugliness of the situation and win us all over and we will be okay with them being together. She doesn't seem to know she's run out of options.

"Maybe if I can get out of this place, I'll go back to Pikes and…"

I shift my gaze to the ground and she stops.

"Well, you'll see." She senses my disapproval. "It will just take time to smooth it all over. He goes through these episodes."

A bell chimes and the health aide at the door signals for us to come in. As we get up from the bench I turn to see the koi pond. The fish are back to being red and black. As we leave the courtyard through the door, I turn again and this time the fish and their pond have vanished, as if they exist only when in the presence of others.

Kevin and I return to his car and begin the ride back home.

"Hard to see Mom like this." I don't know why he is calling her Mom. Tactic, my attorney would likely say. Play along, she'd say.

The highway is dark. Nothing has changed, I tell myself. My mother has not really changed. She is on the edge of the same cliff she was the night she stepped into the final chapter of a nightmare of her own making. When things escalated, I wondered what made Buoy bother calling 911. Was it his way of avoiding going to prison? He probably worried if they came and saw a dead body, it would be just as easy to blame him and haul him off for life. If he called 911, there was a chance the state would take her away and maybe he'd be rid of her. Killing her in a different way.

"Can I get you something to eat?" Kevin asks. I am growing sick of his phony gestures.

"Not hungry," I say, wanting nothing of his stale crumbs.

The oncoming traffic speeds by and I count the headlights, taking stock of what I can see clearly. I have left my mother behind for good with my soon-to-be ex-husband who no longer loves me, and I wonder where I lost his love. What did I do? Was I not beautiful enough for him? Could I have done more for him? But I know it wasn't these things. There are bigger things that we couldn't make happen. Things that stalled us—stalled me. I wonder if these thoughts are the same thoughts my mom has when she thinks about Buoy.

Kevin's cell phone is turned face up on the console between us. He has an incoming text. The phone is connected to the car so the incoming text flashes on the dashboard. He scrambles to detach the phone from the car. The text is from Flaire. It's the text he doesn't want me to see.

"Found the right crib. Great price. Can't wait to show you."

A crib?

"A fucking crib!" I yell. "She is fucking pregnant?" I try to yank his cell phone out of his hands as he is fumbling to pull it loose from the cord. He clenches it. I want to reach for something to throw out the window. I want to smash his phone or my laptop or his windshield or something. I want to break things into pieces.

"Mandy," he says, trying to calm me down, and the car is swerving while his words come out jumbled. "I didn't know how to tell you."

We have lost three babies. Three. I do not know who they would have been. I do not know their gender. Yet all of their little faces are clear in my mind. I can see them. I can smell them. Why can't he? I am so angry I cannot cry. I am so angry I start opening my car door. I want to fall out of the car and roll out onto the road. I want to feel all the pain on the outside of my body that I feel on the inside. I want to transfer all of the pain to him. But when I look at him, I know he feels nothing. He is callous and cruel. He is thinking about Flaire. He can smell her hair and visualize her eyes and now he can dream about what their baby will look like. They get to have dreams I don't get to have. He is looking at me, but he only has pity. Like that seed planted in my mom that sprouted dependency, his has sprouted numbness.

"Let me the fuck out," I demand.

"Stop it, Mandy." He swerves off the highway. I jump out and I swear the car feels like it's moving even though he has stopped. I'm standing in tall grass and cars speed past me. In this moment, I don't care if I am hit or not. I want to break his car windows. I want to punch him.

And then I do something really stupid.

I start walking across the highway. Honking horns from cars and trucks demand I get off the road. Kevin gets out and demands I come back. But I don't. I cross four lanes and a median to get to the other side so that Kevin cannot possibly reach me.

His arms are waving and motioning toward the next exit, and I assume he is trying to tell me to meet him up there. I manage to hear him yell, "You can't walk home!"

He zooms off. I assume he knows it's futile to follow me. I wait until I can see he is long gone and then I cross back over.

I walk alongside the interstate, my feet crushing down the overgrown grass and weeds. I dodge beer cans and bottles. I pick up a bottle and sling it into the woods off the highway. I want to toss another. And another. I pick up each and every bottle and toss it, hoping to hear glass shatter. Nothing shatters, though. Duds. All of them. Fuck. I cannot make things nor can I even destroy things successfully.

The walk is long and I am alone. Car headlights illuminate my path. Everything else is black darkness. I am not afraid of snakes or rapists or whatever the hell else lives along night highways. I just keep walking and listening to my breath as I head in the direction of the exit ramp, which is a good five miles up the road. Eventually, I will get there and I will cease making a fool of myself. I will dial an Uber, or a friend when I get to the ramp. But I want to walk this alone. I want to know I don't need Kevin to escort me home. I didn't need him by my side to see my mother, either.

The more I walk the more I feel whatever fear was shadowing me is starting to leave. The more I walk the more I tell this fear I am no longer its goddamn host. I have given up on tossing bottles. I just walk. I don't seem to ever get tired. I just know that in this darkness I feel like I am seeing something—like an apparition. I keep seeing it ahead of me. I keep chasing it yet I don't seem to be getting any closer.

I finally stop and see if it comes toward me. It doesn't. At some point in this odyssey to the exit ramp, it occurs to me that all I really see is what the car lights allow. There is no ghost ahead. There is only space illuminated in seconds by light. And when the light passes, there is darkness again. I never know when the next flash will come but I keep looking ahead. There is only me walking toward an exit ramp about to be divorced from Kevin who is in love with Flaire and not me. They are starting a family and he and I are not. It's a certainty that comes over me as I tire of the walk. It's a certainty that is faintly starting to feel like something I can call the past. My past.

My phone lights up with a text from Kevin. "I'm at the exit ramp. It's too dangerous for you to be out there alone."

Nah, I shake my head. It's not dangerous at all. For the first time I feel safe. For the first time I feel like I know who I am. What is dangerous, I know, is reaching into a pond to touch a koi fish and feeling air between your fingers instead.

MANGROVES

Thickets and pockets of mangroves formed a twisted path. His airboat had broken down in the midst of them and the sun was near set. Nuclear power plant stacks hovered in the distance—the most reliable landmark he'd used thousands of times before now dissipated into the dark. He'd have to walk the airboat back to the house and without the plant in sight, he wasn't sure he could find his way. The mangroves were like mazes melded onto labyrinths, high enough to block distant views. Inside the corridor was like a long-running tunnel that had no end. Where one was going looked exactly like where one had been. Without landmarks, one was left to dead reckoning.

He got out of the boat, tied rope to the bow, and pulled. He was careful. The water was waist-high but it was the bottom of the flats that posed the biggest threat—oyster beds. Sharp edges of shell fanned out all over the beds and one wrong move sliced a foot with the ease of a knife slipping through softened butter. He pondered which was worse—bleeding out in a small refuge bordering the Gulf of Mexico or looking foolish to Sally. She'd probably made her way to the airport by now. He'd look like a fool then to Zell Watkins, his neighbor who told him a million times he needed some kind of communication device with him in the backcountry. But Danny Moody never listened. He was native to the backcountry, he'd say, and refused to have the very thing he was escaping follow him out onto the Gulf.

He was careful to walk-swim so his feet wouldn't touch the bottom for too long. He imagined he looked like an alligator with his head emerging as he tugged the boat through the tannin-colored water. He didn't know for sure where he was going. He thought that as he looked back he caught a faint glimpse of the stacks from the plant. Back in the day before the plant had been decommissioned, one could count on its evening lights to serve as a beacon. It became as permanent as the moon. If what he saw was correct and not just imagination, he estimated he should pull the boat about thirty yards or so before he'd pass the first of three Indian shell mounds. When the first mound appeared he stopped to take off his shorts that were ballooning with water. What if Sally hasn't left for the airport? he thought. If she was there he'd tell her too much time had passed. She needed to go back to Atlanta where she belonged. He couldn't help but recall their last argument.

"No one asked you here, Sally."

"It's only you and me here, Danny. Don't be silly."

She was crazy, he told her. She'd nearly wrecked his life years earlier. You can't just walk back into the things you messed up and think they'll go back to normal. Things were different this time, she fired back. And for what it's worth, she added, things are never normal.

She blitzed a whole new set of circumstances his way: She was finally free. It took longer than she thought. She tried to work things out with her husband, not for herself, but for her kids. It fell apart anyway. Yes, he was a casualty of it. Yes, she was sorry.

He didn't care, he told her. Too little, too late.

"You knew my situation from the beginning," she told him.

"And you knew mine."

He told her his story had not changed. He was a bachelor and that was it. He liked his life—his quiet, his solitude. He liked things in order. Not the "mess" of her life—her kids, her husband, her ailing father, her job that never would cover her bills and her children. He hated her voice, he even told her. He didn't feel the same way anymore and doubted he ever would.

"At least I don't hide out from my messes, Danny," she said, as if she'd settled the argument.

He was quiet. "Low blow, Sally," he said. "I want you out of my life."

He walked out, slamming the door. He blustered his way underneath the house and took his boat keys off the rusted hook that was nailed into the one of the stilts. In a fit, he fired up the blaring motor and caught Sally watching him from the balcony as he spun away.

He stopped at the second Indian shell mound to rest and stared up at the starry night of his youth. With the power plant dimmed, the skies went back to what they once were. He drifted on waters whose patterns he'd memorized—seven rivers crept through the mainland and rolled in currents out into the Gulf. He knew every tributary, knew when to expect the arrival of migrating birds, knew the favorite spots of manatees and what time of day you'd see dolphins.

"Can you show me?" Sally said that first time they met. "The dolphins?"

He looked at her, confused. She'd rented the house next door and had wandered over to him as he worked on his dock.

"My rental came with the use of that little john boat." She smiled. "But I haven't a clue around the backcountry. I'd pay you of course for your time. Or if you know a guide. I just want to get out onto the water just once. I'd be happy with that."

Just once. He now thought differently of those words.

"I'll take you," he said. No, he told her when she asked how much. But she wanted to pay him for his time. No, he told her a second time when she met him at his boat an hour later. Her hair now down around her shoulders and the brim of her sun hat pushed back exposing even more, her brown eyes that glimmered when she smiled.

"You're persistent, aren't you?" he mumbled. She giggled something under her breath. He wondered if that was something she did a lot—giggle. And her voice was a little on the squeaky side. He thought it half cute and, in a way, half not. The airboat motor would solve that dilemma, he thought. We won't have to talk much. He handed her headphones. They powered out of the cove and skimmed the top of the water through mangrove channels. She looked back at him several times and damn if she wasn't giggling the whole time. He picked up speed to scare her a bit. She thought it funny, though. And he found himself cracking a smile. He cut the motor and let the boat drift, then used an oar and pushed his way through a winding channel.

"Haven't the dolphins all been scared off?" she said. "The boat is so loud."

"Nah. Catch'em at the right time and they'll swim along with the boat. They love it. What brings you down to these parts, anyway?"

She wasn't honest with her first answer. Then finally said, bluntly, that she was running away from her problems. More words he'd come to see differently as the years went by.

He drove them closer toward the plant. He knew of a small strip of sandbar the locals called "nuclear beach." She looked in awe as the twin stacks got closer and closer.

"How do you live with that?"

"You get used to it."

"It seems dangerous."

He knew what she said was true. Even though the plant wasn't in use, spent fuel was stored fifty feet beneath the plant's surface and would scare anyone remotely close to it if they thought long and hard enough about all the things that could go wrong. The locals had to make peace with the plant.

"You get used to it," he repeated.

"You must really trust this water."

"Only thing I trust." He fired the up the motor.

They journeyed back toward the cove and he asked her, almost trembling, if she'd like to have dinner. He'd been scalloping earlier in the week and had more than he could manage. The words, as he said them, seemed foreign to him. He'd spent plenty of time with women. But it was sobriety that had become his constant companion. He'd struggled for years and finally eased into an existence of him, his boat and the gulf. Women came in and out like the tide, and he never held on too tight or for too long.

And now, here was this Sally. She was giddy and giggled too much. She revealed, that night on his balcony eating grilled scallops and drinking pitchers of ice water and lemons, that she was leaving her marriage, or so she said. She had children, not young but not grown. And she seemed scattered, at least to him. Nervous energy was a red flag. Signs of uncertainty, he knew. He knew what it was like to get ahead of your thoughts and rattle about when you were trying to mask something.

But he ignored it. He found himself having fun—something he hadn't felt in years that had nothing to do with boats or fishing or being a backcountry guide. He was happy with her around. He told himself the same sorts of scripted lies he had told himself all the years he drank: He was enjoying having fun with a woman he couldn't have. So he wouldn't want her. He'd just have fun with her. She wasn't available, so therefore, no strings. Dilemma solved.

Almost as soon as he bought into this script of his own making, he was sunken into the depths of her life. For the next six months he was drowning in the undertow of her days—the roller coaster of her divorce that teetered weekly with one spouse telling the other to "go ahead and file" yet nothing happened; the lives of her boys that he got caught up in but never met; her stories of her job that she blamed for the impasse of her marriage. It was like her experiences had become a television show that he tuned into every night on the phone that would eventually transition into steamy passionate talk that would linger past midnight. That week of oceans and dolphins and giggling and feeding each other scallops and breakfasts in bed became the bedrock of their romance; the touchstone they reminded themselves of each time one felt the other drift back into the lives they were each anchored to.

"You could move here," he kept telling her. But the boys, she'd say. Her logic zapped him back into reality. It was like consciously drowning and not fighting it. The back and forth and up and down of the relationship and their few brief meetings simultaneously built and wrecked hope. Scotch or gin or rum would numb the pain, he knew. The odors of liquor were starting to tempt in him ways that lay dormant. In moments of clarity, he would sympathize with her. He knew the sort of dependency she was in. Getting out of it was like climbing a ladder. But in Sally's case, he could see she didn't have her hand on the first rung. And the more he tried to help her, the more he could feel himself slipping.

"You'll never understand the maze I'm in," he remembered her once saying.

Try me, he thought.

He got back into the airboat now and grabbed an oar and started to push his way through the channel. It was completely dark at this point, and he questioned his wisdom of leaving the Indian mound. He felt lucky to have found it in the dark, and he didn't have enough light to find his way to the third mound. Maybe he'd be better off just sitting in the boat and drifting through the night, wait for the first shot of daylight. He'd see the power plant and he'd easily get home. He wanted a drink. A drink would make this all so much easier. He wanted to reach into a flask he knew was hidden in a first aid kit he kept on the boat.

He counted the stars in the sky until he drifted asleep, recalling the words he wanted to say but was afraid to. He wanted to have a family with her. With her, he wanted to be a husband and father. With her, he wanted these things that he had convinced himself he didn't want but the truth was he did want them. He feared he couldn't handle them. He had bought into not one, but now two, false stories. He didn't know if he could survive the risk.

He thought of the vision of Sally in his house standing in the shambles of her own failed fantasy. She was now his for the taking. If he did, he'd be a fool. Just like this night in his underwear and t-shirt soaking wet on his broken down airboat in pitch blackness of night in the middle of a mangrove channel he thought he knew his whole life but when tested, he was as lost as any passing tourist. He relied on a ticking time bomb not even a mile away as his best hope of navigating a coast whose tributaries and inlets he knew like lines marked on his palms. He was a fool either way. Freedom was fugitive to both he and Sally. They both struggle with unsettled pasts regardless of what he chose to do. Things are never really normal.

The whiskey was in the first aid kit. It was always there. He took out the stainless steel flask that he'd filled ten years earlier and never got around to removing. He told himself he'd forget about it. Another lie he subscribed to. He unscrewed the top and took a whiff of a scent that took him to a place he could escape decision, escape risk. He let the odor linger, his tongue coming dangerously close to the mouth of the flask. If he went back to this, he'd have his own answer.

He'd end Sally and himself in one swig. But, he could have her now. He thought about the life he had always wanted with her and now, maybe with her, it would be different. But what if it wasn't? What if it was the same messy struggle? She'd always be the boys' mother. The needs of kids never really disappeared. Now she had an ex-husband to contend with. He envisioned more arguments. More muddy details to slog through. More room he'd have to carve in his life for someone else. It sounded like years of compromises. Years ahead of making her happy. Years ahead of figuring out how to build a life together. But it was that word—together—that bore a seed of hope in him. He waited a moment and without thinking he tossed the flask into the water. He'd find his way back through the dark corridors and move ahead. I know the way back, he told himself. He jumped out of the boat and started his trek through the water.

The sound of a boat motor puttered in the distance. As it got closer he could see a light at the front of a small johnboat.

"Well, I'll be god damned." He recognized Zell's voice. "I said I bet I find you out here half naked, lost as a cuss."

Danny stood up and pulled on his wet shorts. "Motor died," he said. "Figured."

"How'd you know to come looking for me?" Danny hopped back into the water and started to tie a towrope to the johnboat.

"Your lady friend came knocking at my door. Woke the dogs up," he said. "She wanted to call the marine patrol. Goddamn, don't bring them into this, I told her. They'll have helicopters out here raising all kinds of hell. I'll find him." He shook his head.

"Sally got you?" he said, realizing she didn't take off to the airport. She must have turned around. Or maybe she never left.

Zell nodded. "She's back at the house. I wasn't sure whether to tell her to stay or go. Figured you had a plan." Zell looked back at Danny soaked and sitting in the boat. "Or not," he added.

Zell fired up the motor and Danny sat at the side of the airboat. He rode back to the cove letting his hand run across the water as Zell picked up speed. He cupped his fingers, forming a barrier as the wake rushed at his hand. It was like he could hold the water tightly, nothing slipping by.

CLOUD COVER

She swells inside of her dress and she can feel the edges of the round, pearl buttons wanting to pop open. She takes it as a sign. At 10:00 a.m. the air is already hot and humid. Florida's August heat builds and builds, starting at sunrise, and this is why she insisted on a morning wedding—to avoid a storm.

"Are you ready?" her grandfather asks.

She doesn't want to worry him. She starts to answer, but then her thoughts drift to an image of her own father, who should be the one walking her down an aisle. He left town when she was a kid. The last she heard he was in Michigan.

Hedda Linden, Timothy's aunt, is the wedding director. Wedding director. Heather thought it was ridiculous to have one. But Timothy is a Linden and they do things this way.

"Music is about to start. Everyone line up." Hedda claps her hands to the right of her face as if to say, "chop, chop." She is a socialite, and one of the sort that likes to mimic famous people, like Jackie Kennedy. Hedda married into the Linden family, and her interpretation of style strikes Heather as odd. She has always noticed the one thing off-kilter in Hedda's interpretation. The pink suit is on point, but a purse too flowery throws it off. A blue tailored dress hits the mark, but a strange straw hat messes it up. Heather stares at Hedda now. She is arranging the bridesmaids in line, telling them to "throw back their shoulders," correcting posture, taming hair, and fixing ribbons on flower bouquets.

Heather analyzes Hedda's floral dress that is paired with a blue hat that sprouts a flurry of blue feathers. Heather stares at it, trying to figure out why anyone would come to a wedding with a fake bird perched on the side of a hat. For a moment, she feels Hedda might be making fun of this wedding. But she knows, this is Hedda. She is trying to fit in. She's not really a Linden. A Linden wouldn't even wear such a hat is what Heather thinks when she looks at it. Maybe that's another sign.

Heather's grandfather bears the expression of confusion, yet he does his best to be engaged.

"Are you ready?" he repeats.

Heather tries to re-focus and be grateful her grandfather is here, but she knows the distance between them more than she knows his spirit. She knows he is doing this because Heather's mother—his daughter—prodded him to do it. He'd been prodded, Heather thought, all the years she'd known him.

So many evenings she'd watch him come home from the hardware store he managed. Heather spent random nights at her grandparents' house while her own mother got back on her feet from whatever relationship she was healing from. After work her grandfather would walk in, tossing his keys on the counter. He always smelled of perspiration and gasoline. If he knew Heather would be there, he stopped at a Quick Mart and brought home a pint of peach ice cream—Heather's favorite. But he'd plop it on the counter with the keys, let out some sort of exasperated sigh, and then retreat to his recliner and not say a word. Her grandmother would serve it to her while she watched television. Then she'd wait for the yelling and the arguing to begin. It usually started with her grandmother expressing frustration with him for not doing enough to make her happy.

"I don't make that kind of money, Della," he'd say. He'd increase the volume on the television as his wife raised her voice until the volume got so loud it escalated them into an argument. What they argued about went in a circular, never-to-be-resolved pattern. It usually centered on their grown children, all drifters in constant states of struggle.

"If you would have supported him, Curtis, he would have never even tried a drug," she'd say.

"Here we go with the goddamned music," he'd shout back. "A

million people are in a band without goddamn support from their parents. Go ahead, Della, bring up travel for Linda and dance classes for Claire. This house. Your car. Bail out Linda from drugs. Bail out Bobby from jail. Bail out Claire from some man. Enough."

It was when Heather's mother, Claire, was brought into the arguments that she paid closer attention.

"Claire can't help herself," her grandmother said. "She picks men just like her daddy."

The sound of the recliner snapped as Heather's grandfather would abruptly take the keys from the counter and leave in a huff. Heather would take her ice cream bowl to the sink and, on her tippy toes, reach up for the faucet to clean the bowl and spoon and quietly put it all back so as not to remind anyone that she was there.

Hedda Linden's head peers out from the church door. She holds up her finger and tells everyone to wait a while longer. Hints of cool air trickle out.

"Problem with the organ," she says. "Slight delay. No need to panic."

Heather feels relief. Hedda moves like a dervish back into the church. One of the blue feathers from the hat drifts into the air as she closes the doors, leaving them all in the heat.

She watches her grandfather. He is staring at the sky. She guesses he is noticing the blue that stretches behind the tapestry of white and grey puffs of bloated cumulus clouds that look like the same shade his hair has become. The clouds are shifting and with each second of morning that slips past, Heather knows they are getting closer to afternoon storms. She begins to feel anxious that if they don't hurry it will rain. The wedding will be ruined.

"Looks like a bear up there." Her grandfather points to a misshapen blob of white, but then she sees the bear clearly.

"A bear in the sky on your wedding day, Heather," he says. "You wouldn't expect that now, would ya?"

Hedda pokes her head out of the church doors.

"Just a few more minutes on that organ," she says. "I'm going to have someone bring you all some water. It's so hot out here." She closes the church door, and a few small blue feathers fall from her hat and onto the ground.

Heather shakes her head. "Maybe it means something good, Grands."

Heather's bridesmaids are all lined up and all in white; a strange choice, people commented, to have all of your bridesmaids in white. But something stirred in Heather when she selected the dresses. She couldn't settle on a color. "It's like she dressed them as if they were alternates," she heard Hedda comment in passing. Heather could now see her point—they resembled Minutemen, ready at a moment's notice.

One of the bridesmaids takes powder from her purse.

"You're starting to sweat." The girl blots Heather's face. "Too hot a day for cold feet." She giggles.

The others fuss over her veil and the train of her dress. But Heather is fixed on the bear in the sky that is starting to shift in shape. It reminds her of a painting—an odd painting of something positioned right in the middle of a landscape. Right where it shouldn't be.

"Look, Grands," she says to her grandfather. "Now it's a fox."

He looks up at the cloud and in seconds it shifts again into something else altogether.

She thinks about one night in particular when her mother was working a graveyard shift at a convenience store. On those nights, Heather was sent to stay with her grandparents. One night, late in the evening, they got a visitor. It was their lawyer, who was also a family friend. She could sense his arrival was expected. It was dark. It was late. And her uncle, their youngest son, Bobby, had not returned home. He was an adult, but lived with his parents. She knows more about him now as an adult, but when she was a child she stumbled onto a book about 12-steps on his nightstand. As a kid, she wondered what it was about. But that night in particular she could recall her grandmother making a point to make sure Heather's favorite shows were turned on the television and that Heather had a bowl of peach ice cream on the table. There were extra things for her to do—a coloring book set out for her with markers that smelled like fruit.

After a knock on the door Mack Jackson walked in, and he took a seat at the kitchen table with her grandparents. Mack had gone to high school with Heather's mom. He'd even dated her for a time back when they were teenagers. He had a son the same age as Heather at school. Mack was considered a "country lawyer" and took on all kinds of cases out of friendship.

Heather tried to stay focused on the episode of The Wonderful World of Disney that her grandmother had turned on for her to watch, but she was just too curious about their conversation. She saw Mack reach across the table and take her grandmother's hands into his. Then he shook his head in sorrow.

"I'm sorry, Della," he said. "We're doing everything we can."

Her grandfather got up and started pacing.

"They really think my son could guard the entire ranch?" he said.

"They're calling him an accomplice," Mack said. "That's what he's charged with."

"How can one small person who is drunk half the time guard an entire ranch while a plane is dropping drugs?" her grandfather said. "He don't even know anyone down in Miami."

"There's more you need to know," Mack said. He took a second and with caution and sadness in his voice delivered what was likely the most upsetting news any plain country folks like her grandparents could receive: "It will be in the paper tomorrow."

Heather's grandmother let her head fall into her hands as tears started to pour. Heather could still hear the characters on the television in the background, but she couldn't tune out the sobs from the kitchen table.

"Why?" she said. "Why does it have to be in the papers?"

Her cries were helpless. Heather could feel the weight of all those sobs transferring over to her grandfather. She could feel the guilt he was taking on. Heather felt guilt, too. If someone could just fix this.

"It's going to be okay, Miss Della," Mack said, standing up. "We'll get through this. You have my word. You're like family, and I'm going to defend him to the end."

Heather watched Mack Jackson walk out the door. She never saw him again. And it would be two years later before her uncle was released from prison and returned to the family home.

The sweat continues to break out from underneath her wedding dress. She wants to slip it off and make a run for it. She looks at her grandfather, still searching in the sky. She thinks about Tim waiting for her inside. He is a nice person. A good person. He is a lawyer. His family has the stability of a glacier. Heather has never ever really fit in with them. She wonders at times what it is Tim sees as a match. As he stands inside the church, she is wondering if he is wanting to loosen his bow tie and step out of his tux. She knows better, though. He isn't. He is ready. She isn't.

"Nonsense." He put his finger to her lips as she tried to utter the words only weeks before their wedding while they went for a walk around the lake behind his house. "Just nerves is all." Heather nodded and went along with what he said. "Everything is arranged. It's all been planned." She feels the weight of this now. She feels the trouble it would cause everyone to change things.

Hedda appears again. "Almost time." More feathers fall from her hat.

This time it is clear to Heather. It is a fake bird in that hat. Here she is with a fox in the sky and a fake bird on her wedding director's hat, all while she is nearly sweat-drenched in a wedding dress that feels like paint dripping off a surface it refuses to stick to.

Her mother is inside the entry of the church where it is air-conditioned and cool. She said she didn't really like the heat and didn't want her make-up looking messy. She steps out now, probably to check on Heather and Heather's grandfather.

"You're doing us real proud," she says to Heather. "Timothy's people are good folks."

Heather nods her head. She'd said those same words to Heather when they had shopped for the dress she is wearing. That day, nothing seemed to fit. Everything looked too white to her, like a shade that didn't exist in real life. It was in the dressing room, when one of the dresses wouldn't button, that she confessed to her mother that she felt like she was making a mistake. The words, unplanned, slipped out but felt like peace oozing from the body when a fever finally breaks. But that peace was quickly met with a fierce warning.

"You can't do that to your family," her mother said. "Not after everything we've been through."

Wrapped in that second was everything she knew—her mother's failed marriages, her uncle's drug arrests, and dozens of other "mistakes" that speckled her family's history. Her aunt's teen pregnancy, which to this day no one had ever really gotten over. Her grandparents' volatile marriage. Mountains of money problems.

She held in her stomach, that day with her mom dress shopping, trying to appear agreeable and comfortable even though the dress constricted her.

"I'll make it fit," Heather said.

"It's time," Hedda says, glowing with light as she pokes her head out the door.

The bridesmaids line up in front of Heather, all of them gazing at her and mouthing in adoring tones, "You look beautiful." This is how it is supposed to be, she tells herself. This is what happens next. She looks at the fabric that has formed her dress and the dresses of her bridesmaids, and then looks at the clouds—all the things in white. It is right now. These things will make it all right now. These are like signs, she tells herself.

"Are you ready?" her grandfather says, as if on a cue, but all the while his sight is still fixed on what hangs in the air.

She takes in a deep breath that she cannot seem to exhale and catches one last glimpse at the fox in the sky that now has shifted again into what looks like a snowy owl. She holds in her breath, tries to create room between herself and the tightness of the dress. She notices that a blue feather from Hedda's hat has landed on her dress. She lifts it from the fabric and runs its edges between her fingers before dropping it. Faint blue, powdery residue remains on her fingers. She feels the dress get tighter and it becomes harder to breathe. She can't stop her pulse from racing.

The church doors look to Heather as if they are flying open. A deluge of white mist unfurls from inside the church and cold air rolls past the bridesmaids, barreling toward Heather, aiming for her as if to claim her for its own with its soft, white fog. The deluge brings a cold that only Heather appears to feel and the dripping sweat that was crawling down her back becomes cool and dry. She stands firm as it blows through her hair, and her dress billows while the multicolored petals from her bouquet start to fall in a flurry of confetti around her. But only to Heather does this happen. She looks at her bridesmaids.

They are unmoved in a perfect line. As if sculpted by ice, their dresses are crisp and still. Their flowers intact with perfect blooms. Heather looks up to the sky. The shapeless clouds are now wisps of smoke. She lets the force of cold air push against her skin and she feels that this force is there for her and her alone; it holds her tight and in its grasp there is silence. Her back straightens tall and she pivots to her grandfather. But he is not there.

There is only Tim.

He stares into her eyes as if he has something to say and he looks to the sky and she wonders if it is up in that space that he will find words and not clouds. But it doesn't matter because words are coming to her. Heather is starting to speak them. Heather can finally feel space between her and the dress. Along his face, small drops of water start to land. He is quiet while Heather finishes the sentence that was cut short at the lake.

BAD SEEING

"We may be miles away, but in the stars, we are connected like a constellation. We miss you all, and we'll see you soon. Love, Marla and Joe."

Blair Corrigan put down the note that arrived taped to a large oversized box that was shaped like a small coffin. Three months into Blair and Brad Corrigan's hasty move to an upscale town a commutable distance from Portland, Oregon, Blair felt like an overstayed guest. Brad's new job wasn't really a career boost. More of a lateral move, although he portrayed it as a step up the ladder. Her happiness for him was practiced. A similar opportunity came his way years earlier, but he'd passed on it. She was happy when he said no.

"I don't want to uproot you and the kids," she recalled him saying at the time. But when it came back around, he accepted it instantly, citing it as a rare second chance. It was much to Blair's surprise. He was intent on the move. She couldn't recall a conversation where she heard him ask her how she felt about leaving all they had worked to build in Florida—friends, school, sports, their home. It was like the decision was cemented in his mind long before he announced it to her.

Blair examined the contents of the box that now sat on top of the kitchen table. She'd moved a potted blanket flower out of the way to make room and the flowers radiated red and yellow, reminding Blair of campfires and pineapples.

"Plant blanket flowers," Marla told her before the move. The week they arrived in Oregon this blanket flower arrived, a gift from Marla, and Blair planned to plant it.

Marla was like that, Blair thought. Marla seemed in tune with the natural world and was always planting things in her yard that would bear fruit or herbs or beauty later. Marla just knew things like that.

Since arriving in Oregon, Blair's thoughts were always drifting back to green lawns of crisp St. Augustine grass where the Metcalf and Corrigan kids built forts and staged faux suburbia campouts underneath a mix of laurel oaks and Sabal palms. She missed living on a street that ended in a cul-du-sac instead of a trailhead. On Facebook, her friends all commented how she was "living the dream" when she posted her new view—a small inlet that stretched to a large bay fringed with fishing boats and rocks and clouds all looking like a Pacific Northwest postcard. She only saw distance, though. This ocean looked gloomy—like if you set sail, you'd eventually tilt off the edge of the earth into an abyss. Nothing like the Gulf, just a half hour from her previous home where they'd join the Metcalfs on their boat in search of sunlit sandbars and small islands. They'd anchor the boat and let the kids loose to swim or hunt for shark's teeth. She wanted the Florida sun on her shoulders while she and Marla Metcalf sat by the pool on Saturdays watching their children make water balloons and devouring drippy watermelon. Their husbands grilled corn and hamburgers and made plans to take the Metcalf's boat out before the tyranny of school schedules, soccer games and homework assignments swallowed their free time. Here, in Oregon, she had no long-term friendships. Here, she was always cold. Their little town came with an ocean view, but Brad's commute to and from Portland left them spending less and less time together. The rain and the quiet drenched her and left her feeling like she was floating, grounded to nothing.

Blair reached into the box and took out segments of an antique mahogany and brass telescope. It was like she was staring at the past. A dread welled up in her stomach. She wanted to toss it immediately. The mahogany was the woodsy reddish brown of fall leaves and was trimmed with shiny brass fittings. The green patina of the cast iron mounting evoked longevity. The whole thing sparkled like a gem. She knew Marla and Joe meant well sending them what looked like an expensive antique that probably had quite a past. It didn't change the fact that she didn't want it. It wasn't the telescope's past that bothered her—it was hers and Brad's, and she felt if she picked up the telescope and looked through it, that is what she'd see.

She was washing and peeling vegetables over the sink for dinner when Brad walked in.

"Look at what the Metcalfs sent us." She motioned with a nod toward the kitchen table, hoping Brad would not be impressed by it.

"A telescope?" he said, admiring the pieces on the table. "Incredible."

"It's so old. No instructions." Blair hoped he'd be at a loss and would want to sell the telescope or donate it. But she knew better. He seemed to not hear anything. He handled each piece gently as he examined it. The look on his face was like he was seeing an old friend.

"Did you hear me?" Blair said. "You won't be able to use it."

He appeared jolted from his thoughts. "I don't need instructions," he said. "I'll put it together when everyone's asleep."

"Don't stay up too late. Kids have a soccer game tomorrow. I don't know where on earth we have room for a telescope."

"I'll find a place," he said, turning his attention back to the all the parts. "I can set this up on the widow's walk tonight."

With this telescope before them, Blair conjured up all the old stories of Brad's childhood and his teen years. The kind of stories you share when first dating. She could see all the paintings of the night sky he'd created in college that she'd once displayed early in their marriage.

Brad had told her that as a child he'd been surrounded by art books. His mom, an art teacher, made it a point to put a paintbrush in the hands of her children. Brad's childhood beamed with colors and textures. No medium escaped him— whether it be clay or metal or wood or paper; his mother kept a home filled with the tools of creation and imagination at hand. One thing that he returned to repeatedly was a collection of art books on their family bookshelf. It was on the pages of these books that he discovered great works of art, some obvious and some obscure. Blair knew it was the night skies that captured Brad's imagination early on. He loved paintings where the sky told a story. And he noticed how light was captured and communicated in paintings. He first noticed this with the work of a painting called Dovedale by Moonlight. She remembered the first time he'd showed it to her. It captured sloping topography while a cluster of clouds opened to reveal a glimpse of a glowing moon. Then there was Moonlit Night by Aivazovsky and his dark and cloudy night sky and a full moon beaming in the distance, almost calling to Brad to come closer, she imagined. And there was Vernet's Night a Port in the Moonlight. Always the night sky. Always the moon. Always the curiosity of what was out there.

He told her it wasn't until his father took him to watch a shuttle launch in the 1980s on a trip to Florida that he became intrigued with "all things space." And the gift of a telescope for his thirteenth birthday cemented a passion with the night skies. But more than anything, it was spotting the constellation Lyra that was forever drawn in his mind. He often quoted his father's words, "Once you find Lyra, you'll never forget it." Lyra was what astronomers called a "double double" star, meaning that there were actually four stars in the constellation.

In college, Brad combined his love of painting and the night skies and became a painter in the same vein as all those painters who inspired him. He was putting his own spin on modern versions of the night skies by painting images taken from the Hubble telescope. He was majoring in art and doing just that when he met Blair.

She remembered it was parents' weekend at college. Brad was dressed nicely because he was with his parents going to lunch. Blair was a friend of a friend who had joined up with them that weekend. They were in completely different majors, different social circles. She wore her sleek blond hair in a bob that he used to say he liked. She was fit—a childhood of tennis carried on through to adulthood. She was so together and self-assured and law school bound. To Blair, Brad looked like a business major when he was all dressed up. This was the image that stuck with her the most—his potential. He was wildly handsome and his blue eyes were visible from across the table where the large group of students were sitting with Brad's parents that day. When she saw him for the first time in his art studio, covered in paint, and hair a mess, it was as if she viewed what he did as a hobby. He certainly won't do this forever, she thought to herself, but never voiced.

Brad didn't seem to think much about the future. She knew of his goals, but in her own thoughts when she was alone, a voice would arise in the back of her mind. Could she really have a life with an artist? Could they raise a family? How would they pay the bills? Before she or Brad could let the answers to these question surface, the swirling clouds of love and sex took over. Blair got pregnant. They both graduated from college, and Brad took a job in sales to support Blair and the baby while he painted at night and on the weekends. Blair put law school on hold. And soon, it was clear to her that she'd never speak of law school again. And Brad painted less and less and seemed to look away from night skies. And they had another baby. And twelve years later they found themselves in Florida where Brad was a top producer in the southeast for medical equipment sales.

Now, with this telescope in front of her, Blair could feel Brad's childhood, his teen years and those stories he'd told her when they were first dating. She could see all the paintings of the night sky he'd painted in college that she'd once displayed early in their marriage, but as their married life evolved, found their way packed in storage.

Brad stayed up late. He poured himself a glass of wine, turned on quiet music, and started to assemble the Metcalf's housewarming gift. Blair caught glimpses as she quietly checked in on him, but he never seemed to notice she was there.

She watched him as, piece-by-piece, he laid out all of the parts. He was slow handling the front lens. He gazed into it from both sides, hoping, she imagined, to catch glimpses of what wasn't designed to be seen. He held carefully in his hands an eyepiece lens mounted at the back-end of the telescope. She could just vaguely recall the early days of their relationship when he once tried to explain to her the purposes of each part of a telescope. But at the time, she remembered it all sounding like babble. Something about an eyepiece controlled the pathway to the something. She remembered the word "counterweight" because she knew immediately it wasn't the sort of thing she felt necessary to know or take note of. He was sliding something up and down like he was trying to balance the telescope in his hands. He sipped his wine slowly and piece-by-piece she saw the parts come together to complete the finished telescope. But it was his smiling through the process that bothered her the most.

Once she heard the rain from outside, Blair knew it wasn't a night for stars, and wondered where he'd put the telescope. She watched from the top of the stairs as he placed the telescope in the center of the living room's bay window overlooking the Sound. Why there, she thought? From the window bench, it was the best view of the sea. It was Blair's favorite spot in the house. He aimed the telescope to what looked like a specific spot. Blair almost spoke up to announce her presence and ask what he was looking at, but something inside of her already knew the answer.

"With the eye you see one star." Brad quietly repeated his father's words in what he must have thought was to himself. But Blair heard every word, and remembered from whom he'd learned them. "With binoculars you see two. With a telescope, you see four. You'll never forget it once you find it."

She imagined he took pleasure in the thoughts of the many nights ahead where he could explore constellations that were gateways to more stars, more lights, more planets, more exploring, more possibilities. He left the telescope in the window and finally went to bed.

"What if we put the telescope in the kitchen?" Brad asked her the next morning while she poured his coffee. "Just for their visit."

"That won't work either." She scrambled eggs for their boys who were getting ready for school. "It won't work where it is now, though. I can't see the water."

"We could try to put it in one of the kid's rooms," he said. "The boys would think it was cool."

"Their rooms are crammed," she said. "If we move it from the window, you can't get around the chairs. If we put it up against the opposite wall, it covers the fireplace. It just doesn't fit anywhere." She began to pack the kids lunches for school. "You were up awfully late. Were you using the telescope?"

He sipped his coffee, reading the paper. "Yeah, tried too. Bad seeing."

"What do you mean 'bad seeing'?"

"Astronomy talk. Couldn't see a thing, really. I say we just leave it where it is for now, even though I know you hate it there, and then we'll deal with it when the Metcalf's leave." Maybe he hoped the telescope would just fade into the background and maybe Blair would forget it was there.

"I guess," she said, scraping remnants of burnt eggs into the disposal. "Who gives someone a huge thing like that anyway?" She flipped the disposal switch and thought about how Marla used a compost pail next to the sink. Blair had started using one as well under Marla's influence. But Blair had always found it inconvenient. She looked at the pail now sitting unused on her counter. It went into that afternoon's trash.

"It's just stunning," Marla Metcalf said days later, as she and her husband Joe walked through the house admiring the distant views of water, fog and clouds. Marla looked like light standing in the room where the telescope was positioned in the bay window. Messy, auburn ringlets framed her face. Even in the chilly weather, Marla's clothes looked gauzy and light, two undone buttons exposing freckled cleavage. She practiced yoga daily and her energy was always positive and upbeat.

"Takes some getting used to, I suppose," Blair said. "I'm happier now that you're here." Blair felt like their old life had arrived, and she was transported over the next few days to all they had left.

They made meals together, drank, smoked, and laughed. For four glorious days Blair felt like she was herself again, back in Florida, moored to friends and memories.

The last night of the Metcalf's visit they all stayed up late into the night.

"I love where you put the telescope, Blair," Marla said. "Everyone enjoying it?"

"Yes, yes," she said, caught a little off-guard, hoping her dislike for the telescope didn't peer through. "Brad put it together the day it came."

Joe Metcalf spoke up. "I tried to steer Marla toward something more modern. You know," he said excitedly, "they make telescopes that you can hook up to your phone? But Marla picked out this antiquated thing. I didn't think it would work. Marla just knows, so I go with it."

"She does," said Brad, and Blair saw that he tried to avoid eye contact with Marla.

"Have you used it?" Marla fixed her eyes directly on Brad.

Brad nodded.

"He uses it all the time," Blair said. "He loves it, actually. He did a lot of star gazing growing up, didn't you, honey?"

Again, he nodded.

Marla stood up. "Show me, Brad," she said, walking over to the telescope. Blair nudged at Brad to be a good host.

She watched him at the telescope and asked Joe about his boat and how fishing had been and their kids. As she continued with her questions, Blair was struck by something she hadn't noticed before. There was a comfort, an ease, in Brad's body language as he stood next to Marla.

"Let me see. Oh, look." Blair could hear, in hushed whispers, Brad directing Marla and aiming the telescope toward what he wanted her to see.

"Haven't had a chance to get the boat out in a month," Joe said, but she wasn't listening to him. His every word sounded like prattling to her. She was trying to juggle keeping up a conversation with Joe, listening to Brad, listening to Marla, and deciphering what was happening.

"Lyra, maybe?" Marla said, smiling warmly at Brad.

And then she noticed it. She noticed it when Brad replied back to her.

"Lyra," he said. "Yes." He smiled, this time directly into Marla's eyes. "I'll show you Lyra."

It crashed Blair like a breaking wave. Lyra. The word she'd first heard back when all of their life stories were the most interesting they would ever be—the beginning of a relationship when the affection blooms like jasmine and rambles over everything in its path. You think it will always stay that plentiful, that fragrant. And sadly, the chapters that follow are never quite the same. The jasmine takes over and you start to regard it like kudzu. The fragrance becomes cloying. Soon you're taking clippers to it and hacking back everything that was once beautiful. A rambling wild bush is exchanged for a hedge.

Unforgettable, Blair now remembered. The word Brad used when he first told Blair about the impression one has when seeing the constellation Lyra. And now, in front of her, Marla was looking through the beautiful antique mahogany telescope at Lyra. Brad's Lyra. How did she know? Blair had never seen the constellation. She never asked him to show her.

And Brad. His posture relaxed like that of a teenager. He slouched, yielded to Marla, and as he stood behind her, sometimes slightly, gently edging her away from the eyepiece to make sure he had it locked on Lyra, Blair could ever-so-subtlety see Marla not budge over but instead lean into Brad, her hair brushing against his check as she looked into the eyepiece, and she could tell that Brad was whispering something to her that only they could hear. To Blair's eye, it looked as if Brad was inhaling an intoxicating scent being so close to Marla. It was brief and you'd have to have your eye fixed on them to see it, but Blair did. And now, to her, the move to Oregon and their new place on the map, seemed to be born of a reason different than that of a job transfer. Anger welled up as she looked at the telescope. It wasn't a housewarming gift. It was a gift to Brad. To Brad, from Marla. The motion of events that she was in felt thick like wet sand covering her—too thick to easily react to by brushing off. Florida taught her that shaking off sand too quickly just spreads it even more. Brushing it off can leave a mess, can make sand fly into the eyes of those around her, like her children. Not addressing it makes one itch. Each granule has to be completely washed off.

"So, do you enjoy astronomy Joe?" Blair said and tried to recover. She awkwardly kept the conversation moving. Joe muttered something about how he was never really into it and added something about fishing.

"But I let Marla make all the gift decisions," he said. "She seems to always know what to get a person."

Yes, she does, thought Blair, her gaze locked on Brad and Marla at the telescope. Brad's telescope. Brad and Marla's Lyra.

In the days that passed after the Metcalfs' departed, Blair and Brad spoke little. Like two glacial rocks anchored deeply in the sea, movement happened around them—the kids, the dog, the routine. The telescope remained in the bay window. Blair anxiously waited for him to move it or dispose of it. She wanted to walk right up to it and toss it through the window, hoping it would reach the inlet and float away. Float right back to Florida. She had days she wanted to take the telescope while Brad was asleep and walk it down to the first dumpster she could find and pitch it. She wanted to take a hammer to it and beat the lenses into shattered into bits on the floor. She imagined Marla walking on those shards slicing open her foot and blood draining from her. But then her thoughts would shift to Brad. This was all his fault to begin with.

Then another deeper feeling began to well up in Blair. It was that seed she'd tamped down so many years ago. And amongst her thoughts of shards of glass and bloody endings, it was that seed that kept pushing its way through. It was Brad. It was Brad who had become lost. Blair couldn't deny her roll in all of it.

"Good to see the Metcalfs," Brad finally said one morning, and she knew he was just trying to cut through the silence.

Blair was reading a book on the sofa. Her window bench still barricaded by the telescope. "I suppose it was."

"Make you miss Florida?" Brad asked.

Blair stared into the book, unable to focus. "I don't know what I miss."

"I guess now that they're gone, we need to move the telescope."

"I'll leave that up to you." Blair flipped a page. "I know you enjoy it."

Brad nodded. "I do."

"And finding those beautiful constellations, like Marla, I mean, Lyra, you would certainly miss."

She let her words collide with the silence. She closed the book, got up from the sofa, and left the room. Brad remained in the silence.

That night, Blair did not go to their bed. The bed was now a confusing place. There had been a growing distance in that space for a while, but she tried not to let it dismay her. "The cycles of a marriage…" She kept recalling the words of older women—her mother, her aunties, women wiser than her passing down lessons about marriage and family and men. How did she not see that Marla was like a satellite circling Brad this whole time?

It was a clear night. Brad stayed up late gazing through the telescope. Blair tried to put herself in Brad's mind. What were the things filling his head? They were likely the things he had long stopped thinking about, she told herself—the Andromeda galaxy, the four moons of Jupiter, the Great Orion Nebula. Those things, those celestial lights and the myths that surrounded them at one time fueled his childhood imagination but now seemed moored to Marla and Blair. When Blair started to think about her and Brad images of money, cars, houses seemed to have crept into that space. Marla was like that star that flickered and kept him thinking of those things that are not things. Blair told herself she should feel comfort in the thousands of miles between Washington and Florida. Marla was not here. And yet, as she'd watched Brad peer through the telescope that evening, Blair knew it was something other than stars Brad was seeing.

It was sunrise when Blair walked into the living room. She thought about going to the telescope and trying to see whatever it was Brad and Marla knew to be just theirs. Blair had not slept. She'd felt pulled into a vortex of swirling water being sucked into a drain. Her mind now flooded with fear and desperation. She thought about salvaging things. She thought about taking a crash course in astronomy so she could show Brad that she sees him, sees who he is. She thought about using the bay window to set up an easel for future canvases and paints.

Her thoughts about doing these things stopped. She did not want to do them. She had no interest in Lyra. She saw paints and canvases as things for the childhood. Things you outgrow. Her old thoughts from college kept twisting around in her. Those were the thoughts that never went away. She couldn't deny that in flickers these thoughts and feelings she was wrestling with were indeed the start of something new, something scary—change. It was a path she feared she might have to go alone. This thought was the scariest of all. Her kids, her life. All of it felt like things might be changing. She wasn't braced for all that this meant. For all the effort she put into envisioning how things might be with Brad if she changed who she was, and if the telescope disappeared forever, that constellation that hung in the night sky would not.

KARST

Louise McRae, my grandmother, is close to passing as I arrive at the Hospice Center in Gainesville, Florida. I enter her room wishing I were walking backward instead.

"Any day now," the nurse said over the phone just a few days earlier. I scrambled to change my schedule at work and took time off that I haven't yet earned. My job is new and I'm young in my career. I didn't want to come. Not because I am sad for my grandmother, which I am, but I feel selfish. I don't want what I believe should be someone else's job. Some years ago, my grandmother listed me as the person who pulls the trigger on all her end-of-life decisions, the kinds of decisions that I have been letting float around me like a satellite in some imaginary universe where an older and mature version of myself exists. The kind of me who could show up on a day like today, a skilled shot, and pull the trigger.

Today is that day. And I am none of these things.

I expect my grandmother's room to be gloomy and depressing, like a crypt in Dracula's mansion. I wish someone was here to hold my hand or do this for me. I hold my breath, bracing myself for whatever odor attaches itself to pending death. I don't want to be here. I want to be back in Tampa with my friends scrolling through our phones and spending too much money on coffee. I want to be planning what I will wear on a Saturday night to a club. I want to be with friends, talking about what time we might meet up at the beach. I want to walk out of this moment and to my car and find myself in my apartment, in my bed, watching movies on Netflix.

I am surprised. Her room is elegant. It is cheery, clean and carpeted. It has a television on the wall. Buttery light slips through the shards of the blue, green and brown glass of a mosaic lamp on a credenza. The light rolls across flower vases, over the sand-colored walls and onto the grey floor. A credenza against a wall holds a pitcher of water, paper cups and a bowl of fruit. There are glass doors with putty-colored linen curtains pulled back and a small patio just outside.

My grandmother is in the bed and her eyes are closed, her mouth open as she sleeps. Yet I expect her to get up and start walking around. Even now, as she is laid out on the bed, she looks strong. Her skin is far from wrinkled. Her legs are slightly exposed from the knee down and there is little atrophy. She is wearing her favorite cotton nightgown that is blue and covered in daisies. She has had it for years and I wonder who knew to bring it. I think she should be buried in this nightgown, but I stop these thoughts and conjure up my mother's voice that would probably suggest something more dignified.

I sit in a rocking chair next to her bed in a spot my own mother should be seated in. The space between my grandmother and me, although merely inches, feels like gaps in eras. My thoughts go to the swirly marble-like surface of a spring, a spring not far from here that my grandmother and mother and I would swim in when I was very young. We'd pack a cooler of fruit and sandwiches and sit along the bank. Just the three of us gazing at the clear water that was like a window to the limestone just under the surface. I was always a little afraid of swimming in the spring—every outcropping mimicked an alligator and every floating twig moved like a snake. And then the splash of my grandmother or mother jumping in would cause everything I saw to ripple and the reflection would change. Reluctantly, I'd swim around but always stayed close to the edges.

What comes next? I keep asking the nurse—oh, I call her a nurse but she might be a health care aide. Aren't nurses supposed to sustain life? Who is taught, and where is it taught, I wonder, how to facilitate dying?

The nurse I pose this question to looks at me as if to see right into the child she knows my adult appearance conceals—and she gives me few, if any, answers. It's like she knows I can't handle it or, by me asking such a question, I've revealed a naiveté.

My grandmother moans. That means pain, right? Doesn't she need more of whatever painkiller they are supposed to be giving her? I am too afraid to ask the specific names of the meds, as if by knowing what to call them somehow draws me closer to my own death. I don't want to know these things. I just want her moaning to stop.

"We've already given her what she needs," the nurse says. My confusion still swirls.

The French doors open and I hear a cough and then my Uncle Cliff crosses the threshold and the ten years that have passed since I have seen him vanish. He seems to drift into the room affected by the looming dread that I sit in. He wears long black shorts, a camouflage jacket and an old grey t-shirt from a Molly Hatchett concert, the shirt likely as old as me. His beard hangs in straggles from his chin and jaw and the toasty brown hair of his youth has now turned the color of driftwood. He has a bandana that is lost in his bush of hair. All that is missing, I think, is a cloud of smoke from a bong that I wonder if I'd find in his car. He laughs as he ends what sounds like a gleeful conversation with people on the patio. He says something to the effect of "you got that right," ending his conversation. And then he sees me.

"Well, looky here!" he says with his arms out to hug me. "Angel girl's come on home!"

He has always called me this: angel girl. I remember the reason, too. After my parent's divorce, my grandmother fiercely hated my father and she carried on a family "hate" campaign against him. Because I looked a lot like my father, she let her hate of him spill out at times toward me. One day, and maybe this was on her worst day, she called me "Satan's child." It was for no reason. She was arguing with my mother about something and this meanness came out in her. Uncle Cliff was there that day. She was no fan of Cliff's, either. She blamed Uncle Cliff (she called him "The High Hippy") for whisking my aunt away from our little hometown. They lived a nomadic life and drifted in and out of town when they needed money. That day he stood up to my grandmother and told her not to ever talk to me that way again.

"Come here, angel girl," he said, consoling me. "Don't listen to your grandmother. She's just a mad old cat."

"Aren't you a sight!" he says now and hugs me. His squeeze is so tight my mind darts back to when he stood behind me as a child teaching me to aim a BB gun toward a grapefruit hanging from a branch, his hands steady on my arm and shoulder.

I start to speak but he takes over.

"Looky here," he says, pivoting to my grandmother. "Can you believe how good she looks?"

My grandmother moans again. She starts to point to the sky. Her eyes are half opened. She will make jerky gestures like this the entire time I am here.

"Yes, yes, Louise," he says, as he holds her hand. "It's your granddaughter."

My mind scrambles with what to say.

"She knows you're here." He smiles at my grandmother, never looking at me.

I wonder how that is possible. I want his kind of certainty. I think again about how when he taught me to shoot, he started me off with aiming for grapefruits. Once I got good at that we moved on to tangerines. And once I got good at that he moved me along to what would be the hardest aim—kumquats.

"No different than the grapefruit," he'd say, helping me point the gun toward the two-inch fruit dangling from the tree. "Your mark is the same size on both objects. Lock in on it. Trust your aim."

"Does she need more pain medication?" I ask him.

"Nah," he says, "they just gave her some."

We step out into the hall. He has been absent from all of our lives for years. I saw him when my mom passed and he came to her funeral, and I know that was ten years ago.

"Where have you been living?" I ask.

"Well," he says, looking away. "That is kind of complicated." He smiles and answers like he is talking to someone else. "Out west mainly." He makes eye contact with me and then lowers his voice to an intimate whisper: "On a voyage."

A voyage. I picture my mother and grandmother rolling their eyes.

"Boulder," he continues. "Had to get out of that place. Too many people. Hung out in Taos for a while, then I camped around some reservations. Hung out with that crew."

Like I'd know who "that crew" was. I think back to all of the "voyages" he'd taken throughout my youth. He took my aunt away from our small town—a marriage my grandmother disapproved of. He and my aunt would disappear and then reappear. They'd camp, stay with friends, lived in a tipi and then a yurt before yurt's were trendy. The voyages took a toll on my aunt. The call of disappearing was too strong of a pull for him, and then like smoke, he was gone, leaving my aunt behind.

"Aren't I supposed to sign some papers?" I say this hoping he'll tell me "no." I hope he will volunteer to handle the whole thing for me and that I can leave. But he doesn't answer. I cannot understand why I am getting no answers in this place. I want to complain to someone. I start to feel like I am sounding like my mother.

"Let's get some food," he says and ushers me down the hall. Everyone who passes us knows him. The staff smiles when they see him. "Well, hey Millie." He hugs a woman who I presume to be a nurse. Then, "Hey, Mr. Thompson," he says to a janitor as the man shakes his hand. Uncle Cliff pokes his head into a room down the hall from my grandmother's and makes eye contact with a woman who is tending to her own dying kin. He smiles and a makes a quiet gesture of placing his hand over his heart and then kisses it, motioning toward her. She smiles and I see what looks like gratitude come across her face as she nods her head and mouths "thank you" to him. He seems to know everyone in the Hospice, I think.

"They've had it real bad," Uncle Cliff says to me. "That's her son in there. Parent shouldn't have to bury their child."

His candidness burns me. My own grandmother lies in a bed dying and she too has buried not one, but both, of her daughters. First, my aunt, Cliff's wife, died in a car accident while he was off "voyaging." Then, ten years later, my mother succumbed to an illness that swiftly moved through her system and gave us little, if any, time to process it all. While both daughters' actual deaths were swift, for my grandmother it plagued her every day. Mom's friends kept giving me items to remind me of her—mementos they had of her or a heartfelt letter they wrote that they assumed I'd want to read and that would help heal me. All her things became mine. My grandmother wanted to me to stay in our town, but as soon as I got the chance I slipped away before her expectations tattooed me forever.

"They have the best chicken salad," Uncle Cliff says as he leads us into a small kitchen. He opens the refrigerator like he's in his own house. I wonder who'd want to eat this "death food" at a Hospice? Yet I find myself accepting a paper plate with a few finger sandwiches and a Solo cup of sweet tea and soon I'm am stuffing my face with Hospice food. I am surprised that I like it.

"Yesterday someone brought in a pound cake and, oh!" his voice howls, "that was million-dollar eating!" He stretches out the word "million" to make it sound like he's in ecstasy. I worry others hear him and think we we're celebrating, but he is not concerned.

"Kooky" my grandmother used to say about Uncle Cliff.

"She's been waiting for you," he says. "I wondered if you were coming. I knew this would be hard. I wouldn't blame you for skipping."

My grandmother had been sick for a long while. She'd been in a nursing home. I kept hoping she'd die when I wasn't looking. Like a fluke with no time to react. But she held on. I felt like she was waiting for me.

I came to see her very little; something that makes me feel guilty. I resented both of her daughter's dying because, to me, it rushed my own life. I wanted to stay young. I didn't want to think about what it means to be old. Being old is something my aunt and my mother will never know. And seeing my grandmother old and dying made me hate her. Why should she get to have lived for so long?

When my mother died, I remember something that a friend of hers said. It was the one "memento" I couldn't seem to leave behind no matter how far I traveled. That friend hugged me and then whispered: "Now you will take her place." It was like she was laying a curse on me. In that moment, my teenager self started plotting an escape plan. But later, I learned that I was named in my grandmother's paperwork as being charged with all kinds of responsibilities that would ultimately draw me back.

When I walk back into the hallway, I see a familiar figure walking toward me. It's Bobby Michaels. He is a friend from high school, but not just any friend. His father used to date my mother when they were in school. I haven't seen Bobby in at least ten years.

"Sunny!" He gives me a hug. "Sunny" is a nickname that he gave me because we were the sun and moon, respectively, in a childhood school play.

"I heard about your grandmother," he says. "Dad thought I should come down here and check in on you. He was worried you'd be all alone. Hope it's okay that I've come."

I used to think of him as the brother I never had, and I used to wonder what my life would have been like had his dad and my mom married. Of course, it was silly. We both wouldn't be here. We'd be different people. But it was a version of him—brother—that I never really shook.

He and my uncle exchanged pleasantries and my uncle went back to my grandmother's room. Bobby and I walked down the hall together and found a bench where we could sit and talk.

"Is there anything Dad or I can do for you? He was worried about you. He wanted to offer to come down here and help you with all of this. But he didn't want to overstep. You know how special your mom was to him."

That specialness between him and my mom was also a source of contention between my mother and my grandmother. It was another misstep my grandmother was always reminding her of: she should have married Larry Michaels.

I take Bobby through the series of events that led to my grandmother being here. He listens to me intently. He places his hand on mine as I talk about it. Bobby is a man now. He is handsome and I ask myself how I ever saw him as a brother. He is an environmental engineer, which I knew. And he is unmarried, which I also knew but now take special note of. I am here for my grandmother's passing, but sitting with Bobby I am smiling and distracted. I want to pass the night with him and drink and laugh. I want us to linger in the bar having too much fun and take things a step further so I can remind myself that we are not, nor have ever been, related and that it was my foolishness to begin with to feel we were. I sense he wants to do the same thing with me. I remind myself that I'm in a Hospice facility. I'm here to help my grandmother die, a grandmother that I'm conflicted about. I want her to pass, but not be my responsibility. I want her to pass, yet I also want her to jump up and swim in that spring. I want this because I know that if she does this, it would mean I was a child again. And my mother would be swimming in that spring, too.

I abruptly stand as I see a nurse walk toward my grandmother's room and Bobby walks down the hall with me.

"I can wait out here if you want," he says. I take his hand and walk him inside. He lingers in this space with me. I'm not sure why I led him in here, but he doesn't seem to fight it. He stands with me, his arm draped across my shoulder, and waits. We wait together for minutes more and then I turn to him.

"I should just be here alone."

He nods and takes out a business card from his wallet and a pen from inside his jacket. He writes his cell number on the back and lays the pen and card on the credenza.

"Call me when you are ready," he says. We hug and he departs.

After a moment I realize my uncle is standing behind me. I want to take a few minutes to look at her. She has aged well. This death that is hovering over her is from a deterioration of her mind. So much about her says she could still live on. So much is still in working order. I try to reconcile this with the fact that her mind is what has failed her. And in this room have passed three people who are probably the last three she would have expected to be at her deathbed.

I try to put myself in her mind and body, and wonder how she got through the loss of her daughters. I reach for her hand because I'm hoping that a bit of my mother can seep through the ends of my fingers and touch her. I want to heal a small part of that pain that I know, when I am older, I might understand as I take the risk of loving another person more than myself.

I let go because I get scared that maybe I might actually feel that missing piece of my mom I wanted to know more, that part I wish was here right now. Why isn't my mom here right now? She is supposed to be here, not me.

My grandmother's mouth opens and I remember that there is water on the credenza. I'm compelled to give her some. But I don't think I am supposed to. Where are the nurses? I feel like we should stop all of this. I see her strength and her potential to live just a little bit longer. Is it not evident to everyone else?

I feel my uncle's hand on my shoulder.

"It won't be long now, angel girl," he says to me.

I'm confused. I'm here to do a job, and I stand up and walk out the door to the nurse's station. I explain I'm her granddaughter and I'd like to see a file or whatever it is I am supposed to sign. I want to save her life and at the same time, I am charged with ending it.

I feel my uncle's presence behind me.

"I'm supposed to approve of all this, aren't I?" I say to him. He says nothing to me but puts his hand on my cheek. His lips stretch to a smile but his eyes move toward the floor, as if he doesn't want to interfere.

The nurses have pulled her file. I flip through pages, and pages scanning them, looking for my name. Her wishes are clearly spelled out. She has made all of her own decisions. All that is left to do is sign off on everything. I take the file back to her room, and a nurse and my uncle follow.

"I can sign your name if you want," my uncle says to me. He reaches for the pen Bobby left on the credenza.

I am holding onto the folder tightly, not wanting to turn it back over, not wanting to let it go. I go to open it again and think that there has to be a mistake. There is no getting around this. The nurse is patient and as I start to re-open the file, I fidget and my mind wanders—springs, tangerines and gunshots and a cardboard sun costume. I see my mother's face, my aunt's face. I picture Bobby and me as children. I stop the barrage of images in my head. It's time. I take the pen from my uncle's hand and sign my name on every line where it is printed and hand the file back over.

My uncle and I walk back into the room and he turns off the television. He turns off the lamps. I know after today, I will likely not see him again. Voyages will call him back and he'll take to the road.

I take my place back in the rocking chair and reach out to find my grandmother's hand. I decide, yes, she will be buried in this nightgown. It is the most fitting for her. Without light, without sound, without water, there is soon no longer a gap between us.

Hours pass and it is just me alone in the room. My uncle has left. The nurses are gone. My grandmother has been wheeled out. They tell me to stay as long as I need. I soon discover that the moments after a person passes are in their own realm that feels like a bubble of air that has been pierced. The air you inhale after these moments have to be made up of something more than science. I think the air that fills this space that I am now breathing is a certain type of air that my grandmother was robbed of after both her daughters passed. It's an air that my mother and aunt will never know.

I remain in the rocking chair and I let the emptiness of this room settle in me. And eventually, the moments shift into a new time where she is now in the past.

I get up from the chair and decide it is time for me to leave. I walk through the door and I think about the spring. I will swim in it before I leave town. I will swim underneath the surface and past the twigs that look like snakes. I'll grab a twig and let it skim across the surface of the water as I push it out of my way. I'll swim to the outcroppings that look like alligators and see what they are really made of.

HONEYCOMB

He was there to clean the ashes. His clingy black bodysuit was speckled in dust and soot. He smelled of smoke. His name was Edge, and he walked through Beth's kitchen straight to the fireplace like he'd been in her home before and needed no one to lead him.

Beth was preparing food for guests when he arrived. It was her turn to host the card game. She'd put off having people over because she'd been keeping her difficulties a secret—her troubled marriage and now it's official ending. She was waiting for the right time to tell her friends, but when no one replied to her e-mail reminding everyone about card night, she worried that word was out. Maybe the quiet response was due to the fact her friends felt hurt that she hadn't told them herself. She wasn't ready—to tell it or to live it. She had been going about her activities as if still married and wore her ring every day even though she would take it off as soon as she walked through the door.

She decided she would arrange cheeses and meats and fruits on a wooden board and nestle slices of honeycomb and bread throughout the tray. She prepared it with the assumption, the hope, that they would all arrive.

The chimney sweep worked her in last minute. It had been Beth's intention to clean up the fireplace from the weeks of her incessant burning of things. As the pace of divorce had escalated, she'd taken to gathering and burning all she could find that had to do with him—

photos, a diary she kept from when they were dating, concert tickets from their early years.

The burning spun out of control. Ashes and ashes piled up and she'd stuffed more things into the fireplace and created more ash. She'd fall asleep by the fire many evenings, forgetting a fire was actively burning. She'd get up the next day and never clean up the mess from the night before.

Despite the heap of grey, remnants of the items that didn't completely burn were still recognizable. Her diary, clothbound, didn't quite burn how she thought. She didn't want the women who were coming to see it wedged at the top of a heap. She didn't want them to see this charred, dirty rendition of her life.

"Burning stuff doesn't make it go away," he said, assessing the tall mound in the fireplace. "Are those club covers?"

They were. She'd gone into the garage days earlier looking for more stuff to burn and discovered boxes of golf tees that easily went up in flames. She'd tossed a box of pricey personalized golf balls in to see what would happen, and they'd burned fine. Beth then noticed his golf head covers. Some were just plain and leather. But one looked like a lion. Beth added it too late when the fire was but embers. The face of the lion survived. It looked like a sad child's toy one finds after a tornado.

The same evening when she burned his golf things, she thought of a special item to burn—his most prized golf possession. With just embers flickering, and with a lot of trepidation, Beth reached for his shadow box. She held it in her hands, clutching it. But when Beth thought about him holding on to whatever-her-name-was, the box flew from her hands into the dying fire. The box contained the ball from his first and only hole-in-one. She'd had it framed for him as a present. When she finally made the decision to toss it, it too burned only half way. The brass engraved plate that included a loving sentiment from her was still visible. Edge got to work to make it all disappear.

Beth now lodged her fingers in the jar of honey and pulled the honeycomb out. It dripped all over her hands and onto the counter as she put it on a cutting board. She started to slice through the comb that was about as long as a bar of soap. The hexagonal holes ran in a pattern the length of the comb. Each hexagon was symmetrical to the next. Perfection. She thought about what her DNA strand would look like all spread out on the wooden cutting board next to the perfect hexes—twisted ladders of cell matter. She wondered if deep inside the hexagonal holes she'd find imperfections like adultery and anger. Would she find piles of ash left behind by a Queen Bee who was no longer needed at the hive?

Beth finished slicing the comb into bite-size pieces and placed them around the fruit and bread, but as she scrutinized the pieces she didn't like the appearance of the honeycomb. The pattern bothered her. It reminded her of the skin of reptiles coyly making their way through grass. She imagined the cold wet sensation of a racer snake sneaking up on her in her sleep and the horror that would come over her coming eye-to-eye with it. The knife then slipped and cut into her finger, her ring finger, that was holding the comb steady. Teardrop shaped beads of blood dripped onto the honeycomb. She put her finger to her mouth to stop the bleeding and turned on the faucet to run cold water over her hand. She slipped her wedding ring off under the faucet while cold water and blood dripped over it, and then she wrapped the ring in a paper towel and put it down on the counter. She'd worn her wedding ring as part of a routine she'd adopted when around her friends. Now she made a mental note to put it back on before they arrived.

She looked down at her finger. Nothing bad once cleaned up, but her blood had ruined the honeycomb.

"Pro tip." The message popped up on her phone. "Never give out your last name." It was from a guy Beth knew only as Ted from a dating app called Stage. Online, she was "Bex." It was one of the ways she now passed the time, another secret kept from her friends. She didn't remember giving him her number, but she must have told him her last name. The phone dinged and when she looked at her screen a photo of Ted's penis appeared. She should have been alarmed. How did he get my number? she asked herself. She zoomed in on the photo to examine his penis. It wasn't the first such photo she'd received since dabbling online. She was getting accustomed to the photos and less startled when they suddenly popped up. She left the phone, face up, on the counter.

"Can you make it all go away?" she asked Edge. "It's a lot of ashes."

"Sure." He said. "Ashes are the easy part." He shook his head, looking at the pile that was before him. He had a vacuum and plugged it in, then put a mask over his face.

A ring sounded at the door, and Beth saw through the window that it was Denise. Denise was a tattoo artist, a single mom. She partied and drank and her arms were covered in black and white tattoos. She and Denise had dramatically different lives. They'd met by chance at the liquor store.

"I wouldn't buy that garbage," Denise had said in the store and nodded toward the flavored vodka Beth was about to pull from the shelf. "Hardly a buzz from that shit." Denise bent over to pull a large jug-like bottle from the bottom. "This is cheaper." Somewhere in the shuffle of walking down the aisles of the liquor store, a connection sprung.

Denise later took Beth to bars, taught her about online dating, introduced her to men Beth would never really be interested in but helped her pass the time as her marriage unraveled, men who weren't seeking anything permanent. Men who liked to please women but didn't want to commit to them. Women were hobbies to these men.

And now, Beth looked at her ex-husband's hobbies that formed a ridge of cinders.

She wasn't prepared for Denise to show up, had not invited her. Beth's card group was all married moms. If they saw Denise at her house, they'd think she'd gone wild. Beth opened the door and Denise was a mess, tears causing her bronze make-up to drip down her cheeks exposing ruddy pink skin.

"What's wrong?" Beth said, putting her arm across her shoulder.

"That asshole," she said. "That's what's fucking wrong."

Beth brought her into the kitchen. It was the latest in a string of men Denise thought would be "the one." She always had dates. Lunch dates, dinner dates. Beth couldn't keep them straight. Denise's men all melded into one composite that Beth conjured up looking like the leader of a biker gang.

"What did he do?"

Denise launched into a fit of anger about the latest transgression. Beth put her arm around her. Denise had done this many times for Beth, too, wrapped her tight on those sad nights when Beth would have been on the floor had it not been for Denise whipping her into getting dressed and meeting her at a club. Beth would feel out of place and dressed in clothes a mother would wear. She'd drink and drink until she was loose enough to get on the dance floor or talk to men she'd never seriously want to be involved with. It was her new life. And Beth hated it.

The sound of Edge's vacuum fired up.

"Someone here?" Denise asked from her sobs.

"Chimney man," Beth said. "All of Ed's shit I've been burning."

The burning had been Denise's idea originally.

"I didn't think you'd burn everything in the goddamned house," Denise said when she looked and saw how tall the heap was getting.

Edge breezed past the two women as he carried the remnants of the shadow box.

"Where are you taking that?" Beth asked.

"Truck," he said.

"You can't keep that," Beth said. "It was supposed to burn."

"But it didn't," he said.

"It's mine." Beth stood up.

Then Denise stood to intervene. "I can take the box to the trash."

Edge lifted his hand, motioning Denise to step back.

"You don't want it," Edge said, directing his gaze to Beth. "It won't do you any good anyway."

Beth looked at the half-charred box in his hand. The ball was misshapen, indented in the middle and supple like it was on it's way to charred ash. Beth put her hands on what was left of the box.

"But what if I want to save it?" Beth said.

"You don't."

"What the hell, Beth?" Denise said. "What are you going to do with it anyway?"

Beth wanted to rip the box out of his hands. But she didn't. His mouth was still covered in the mask, and his eyes appeared beady and prominent to her against his balding head. Her gaze was locked in on him. Beth released her grip. He took the box and walked out to his truck.

"Can I hang out here with you a while?"

"Of course," Beth answered without thinking and watched Edge through the window as he tossed the box into a trailer that was piled with trash bags Beth imagined were filled with ashes from other homes.

The ladies, Beth realized. They'd be coming soon, or not. And there was Denise. Where to put her? She heard her phone ding again from the kitchen, and she imagined a never-ending stream of penises coming across her phone while she was trying to entertain her friends.

"Actually, no," Beth said to Denise, trying to backtrack. "I've got all these people coming over."

"I can help you get ready," Denise said. Her damp eyes seemed to ask for pity. Beth tried to consider what the ladies would all think when they walked in and there was Denise, the wildest of the bunch. They'd know she was wild, and have no idea what Beth was doing with her.

"Wait, stay," Beth told her, a kind of defiance rising within her. "Yes, you can help me set up. And stay late if you want."

Edge had come back inside and was finishing his job. He now went to the kitchen faucet to wash his hands, and he reached for the crumpled paper towel on the counter, let it soak up the water from his hands and tossed it, still crumpled, in the garbage. Beth watched him and some voice told her she was supposed to remember something about the paper towel. But her phone dinged again, distracted her, and she went to reach for it, but Edge beat her to it. As he held it in his hands he smirked at the photo coming across the screen. He then laid it back down on the counter shaking his head in disapproval of Beth as he left the screen facing up. She felt as if he was looking at her undressed and exposed. She went to reach for the phone but stopped as she stared at Edge looking at her. She felt that he was seeing an image of her she couldn't capture in a photo or in a mirror. The kind of image that peels the portrait off the paper and places it into a context giving it a truth that voids out the paper image rendering it little more than the facsimile it is. She exhaled, letting calm take over. Her hand retreated and she left the phone facing up.

She realized her hands were still gluey from the honey that had not yet dried.

They stood at the counter where Beth had the food arranged artfully on a platter. She looked at her hands and noticed ash from the shadowbox had stuck to them from when she earlier tried to wrestle it away from Edge. Beth went to wash the flecks of ash from her hands just as the doorbell rang. She could hear Denise say she'd answer the door. Her phone dinged again. Beth wanted to beat Denise to the door and at the same time put away her phone, but she looked at the counter and noticed the one imperfection to the food she had arranged on the platter. She had yet to dispose of the honeycomb. Her blood had now dried on it. She looked up from the honeycomb and noticed a look of intrigue on Edge's face. Beth watched him eyeing it. He lowered his head to smell it. He poked at it, turned it around and around; leftover honey oozed out of the hexagonal holes mixing with flaky bits of her dried blood.

"Don't touch that," Beth said to him.

His eyes never left hers as he picked up the bloody honeycomb and began to chew on it.

She watched him looking at her as his face conveyed pleasure savoring her dried blood mixed with sweet, pasty honey. She slowly made her way toward him and put her hand on top of his, letting her hand slowly move up his arm, feeling the slickness of his body suit as her long fingers reached his lips. She let her fingers slowly catch a drop of blood and honey that dripped from the edge of his mouth. She put her finger to her lips and licked it, smiling, like it was candy.

FIRST TATTOO

When he took his shirt off, it was in the back room of my studio. I had him come by early in the morning so we could go over the art he wanted for the urn. When I stood before him and looked at his chest and arms, I was a little overwhelmed with the number of his tattoos.

His chest was covered with what looked like a half dozen, but they had been applied in such a way that they melded together, blurring lines. I decided to keep index cards on each tattoo and take notes about each one to decide how and where each would be applied to the urn. As he sat there, bare-chested, on a stool at my work table, I stood beside him sketching out ideas and taking notes. In the studio's light I could see his face more clearly than at the bar a few nights before. He was tall, but not remarkably so. He had a medium build. His skin was that warm tan folks in these parts attribute to Cherokee roots somewhere in their background. His hair was shaggy, silver and black, and thick. He was muscular, and I found myself working a bit at staying focused.

A few nights earlier when I met him at the bar he said his name was Ray.

"Erica," I said in response that evening as he took a stool.

"Nice work at your shop." I was taken aback that he knew the studio and couldn't recall him amongst the tourists that flowed in and out.

"Thanks." I placed his beer on a coaster in front of him.

"You been doing that sort of thing a long time?"

I shrugged my shoulders. "Kind of, I guess. It's all I really know, besides bartending."

"I like it," he said and he lifted his glass to me. "To what you know."

I smiled. "Ray short for Raymond?"

"Reinhardt," he said. "German mother."

"I like Reinhardt," I said, wiping down the bar space near him. He sipped his beer.

"I like Erica," he said, looking around the bar and not really making eye contact with me. Yet he stayed until the bar nearly cleared out. Then he said there was something he wanted to ask me, could I make something for him. Custom.

"It's not just any vase I need," he said. "It's an urn. For ashes."

"Whose ashes?" I asked.

"Mine."

"I see."

"Can you do this for me?"

"Let's start with that owl," I said now, motioning to his upper right shoulder and also trying to jolt my focus back to the getting of what I needed to create the urn. I'd have to photograph each tattoo and then create a transfer decal based on the photo. The decal would be applied to the urn, in essence "tattooing" the vase.

"Is that one you'd want on this?"

He nodded. "Yeah, I'd want this on there."

I picked up my camera and photographed it, then I jotted down the word "owl" on a notecard. I wanted to ask him why the owl and what it was about, hoping it could help me decide how to prioritize where to eventually place it on the urn. But the whole thing was awkward. Here was this half-dressed man in my studio, wanting me to create this elaborate tattooed vase for his ashes. I sat staring at his chest and arms covered with art. Swirls of colors and years of memories branded onto him. It was now my job to peel each layer of life from those experiences and tell his story on clay; something I'd been not only trained to do, but an art form I had practiced every day. And yet, now I was as lost as those blurred lines that enabled his numerous tattoos to appear as one.

"Okay, let's go on to the next one," I said. There was a bird of some sort on the other shoulder. But my eye went to the red dragon on his chest. "You'd want this one, right?" I asked, motioning with my eyes toward his chest.

"Yeah," he said, "that's my battalion crest."

"Army?" I asked.

He nodded. "Vietnam. Two tours."

I snapped a few photos. The sound of the shutter filled the awkward silent moments.

"I don't think we can fit all of these tattoos," I said, walking behind him to see all of the ones on his back. A hula girl, flash art that was common back in his younger days, was wearing a banner with word "Liar" accented with a sun on the end of a banner.

"Why Liar?" I asked.

"It used to say Linda," he said. "I had it fixed when I found her with my best friend."

I laughed. "I'll assume you don't want the liar tattoo on your urn."

"We can skip that one," he said.

One by one I photographed his tattoos. When he left I flipped through my notecards. An owl with talons. The red dragon. A brown bird. The coiled snake on his back. The Mexican woman next to the red dragon on his chest, amongst many others. All of these images I wondered about. I sketched out the urn and did rough outlines of where I would place each tattoo. I played around with the arrangement of all the images but felt like I needed more input from Ray with regards to the significance of the tattoos. This whole project was my idea, my doing. He'd just wanted a simple cremation urn, and I was turning it into my own little art project.

While I was intrigued with the randomness of him floating into my life, I needed to knock out about a dozen or so mugs, a teapot and a creamer set, and a handful of soup bowls. My busiest season— leaf season in these mountains—was a narrow window closing in on me. I counted heavily on those few weeks of gloriously decorated mountain sides in a riot of all the colors of decaying life—burnt orange, sienna, chartreuse, bronzy cranberry red. I captured those colors in my work in a way that, hopefully, resonated with visitors to my studio enough times to insure I'd make it through another long lonely winter. My life was like this now—getting through seasons. I dreaded winter. Always uncertain I'd make it through–the rent, my car, insurance, food and slow-as-hell sales. Hardly any visitors. The locals hunkered down, watched their pennies, and stretched soup to make it work until the spring opened her doors and let people and money flow back in.

I took off what little jewelry I had on before sitting down to the wheel, an old habit taught by my first pottery teacher: Anything hanging from you can be your undoing. I laid my bracelet on the table and started to take off my necklace that had an artist's friend's rendition of the North Star on a chain. I couldn't get the clasp undone so I skipped it. Just this one time, I told myself. I laid the bracelet next to a clay ring holder that had not moved from my workspace. A small round sapphire set in white gold sat in the ring holder already. It had remained there for months. I still didn't know what to do with it. He'd insisted I keep it like barter for his guilt-free passage to a new life. I left it where it was.

Crisp, dead leaves sat on a table near the wheel: maple, gingko, oak, fern. I used to know the texture, the veins, the shape of each one like patterns of my own palm. My work, my pottery, was known for how I had incorporated fragments of nature, specifically leaves, onto the surface of my clay. It was joy spending an afternoon along a stream or in a forest sifting through all that nature had distilled and left for scavenger hunters like myself. I would bring my finds back to the studio where I'd craft that discovery into my work, knowing its intention, its purpose, was to leave me and find its way into the hands of another.

But lately, my time at the wheel felt askew. I centered the clay on the wheel as I had been taught to do decades earlier. I was trained to instinctively know the center of a wheel and to know, to feel, when it was time to add or decrease pressure or speed. I was trained to intimately know these things: as a potter centers her clay, so she too will be centered. The clay was now getting away from me more frequently. It was slipping. I was making amateur mistakes. My hands could no longer seem to control the world that was in my palms slick with earth. Those miles I logged for decades at the wheel seemed now like mere inches. I leaned down, forgetting the North Star necklace dangling from my neck, and it caught the top lip of the pot, already shaky in my hands. The speed of the wheel quickly snapped the chain off my neck, leaving a sting as I took my foot off the wheel and watched the misshapen pot slip into a mangled mound of too-wet clay wrapped in a gold chain and a bright star charm dangling off its side.

Ray and I sat at a wood tabletop—still sticky from the previous patrons. A waitress named Rose came by and wiped it down. I nodded to my co-worker behind the bar and he sent over a pitcher of beer.

I still didn't know what Ray was dying from, but there was nothing about him, no actions, no quiver, no glitch in his movements that would indicate anything dire underneath the surface. He seemed in perfect health.

"So you went to war," I said, immediately regretting my words. I was finding myself feeling nervous in his presence and idle chatter was even more difficult outside of the studio where we had a script, a purpose.

"Yeah," he said. Rose put a pitcher on the table. He poured us each a glass.

"How long were you there?"

"Two tours total. A year of combat."

I stopped there. I never know what to talk about with someone who has seen war and death. But it was my own fault for bringing it up.

"Listen, Erica," Ray finally said. "I appreciate what you're doing with the urn and all, but I'm not sure why you want to know all of this about my life."

I didn't have an answer. "I'm an artist, Ray. I don't always know myself."

He lit another cigarette and leaned back into the booth, stretching his arm along the top of it.

"These tattoos tell a lot of stories I'd like to forget," he said.

"Maybe I need to hear them."

I could sense his reluctance.

"We're going with the owl, right?" I said.

He nodded. "Sure, if you want."

"I'm kind of intrigued by it. I did a little research on the meaning of owls—the symbolism of them, and that skull it's covering."

He started laughing again. "Owl's a person," he said, "not some God-damned symbol. You think too much."

We both laughed.

He then took a more reverent tone. "If you've ever had an Owl in your life, you don't need another friend."

Tattoo by tattoo his life's journey unfolded from across the table. Owl? His army buddy who he credited with saving his life during the war. The tattoo of the dark-haired vixen? A former lover from Mexico. The tattoo of the snake? His time spent in the Everglades trapping exotic animals. Each marking came with a story of an adventure, a lover or a heartache. The only story he didn't tell me about was the bird on his arm.

"That bird was my first tattoo," he said. "I'll save that story for later."

We lingered over drinks and food for some time, and finally he looked up at me.

"I'm not seeing any tattoos on you. You have any?"

I shook my head. "No, I've thought about it. But just never did it. I guess I haven't figured out what I'll love forever."

"You'll know," he said and laid cash on the table to pay the bill. "You'll know."

When I could, I would try to blow off steam on a hike. I'd hiked alone most of the time since the break-up. We, my ex and I, used to do some of the more strenuous hikes together, but it was along those times on the trail where our differences would emerge and follow us, hanging in the air like acrid fumes choking out fresh oxygen. It's no way to hike a mountain. He'd want to take one path, I another. He always chose the more punishing route of any crossroads, and when I would resist it would become a war of wills. And it wasn't just directional; it was the pace; it was the length. It was the sheer fact that I'd find myself on an otherwise beautiful day walking a long path through a tunnel of trees and laurels and switchbacks being led by someone who clearly wanted to hike alone. Sometimes I'd loose sight of him on the trail and find myself off trail. One time I missed sight of a white blaze he later said was obvious to everyone else. I had to find my way back to the trailhead parking lot. When I reached my car and looked at a map, I saw that I had veered so far off course that I was in a section the park service deemed too dangerous that summer for hikers due to bear activity. And my ex was actually angry with me when he finally found me. I was convinced what he was really pissed about was that he hadn't been able to shake me off.

Now, I hiked alone to just think and wander and look at foliage and hopefully find inspiration for new work. But lately I'd stare at all those same shards of nature and see sameness. I was loosing my ability to distinguish one plant from the other; colors were starting to just all meld together; the ridges were beginning to soften; the lines too blurred. What would distinguish one species from another was evaporating before my eyes. And I was starting not to care. And nowhere was that more apparent than when I went hiking. Sometimes I'd tune out my own thoughts with music, hoping the rhythms of another's art would just take over my own. I'd existed like this since he left. And I hoped that what I knew of nature—that it regenerates—would take over and solve the state of limbo I was existing in.

On a recent afternoon, when I reached the ridgeline of the mountain I was hiking, I could see the foliage all across the valley, the colors flaming in warm hues across hill after hill. But I had a hard time really seeing the distinctness of the colors like I had for so many years. Like a lost connection on the phone, I couldn't pull up the sound or the tone. Ray's tattoos filled with color and stories crossed my mind as I watched a few hikers snapping photos along the ridge, all seemingly wrapped up in capturing the memory of their shared moments. I thought through the urn and where I would place all his tattoos while I hiked back to the trailhead. I could hear birds off in the distance, but couldn't see them. Again, Ray came to mind. His bird tattoo. I needed to account for it in my placement of the images. Birdsongs accompanied me the entire way to the bottom of the mountain.

The final time we met in the studio for a working visit, I went over all my notes and photos with him.

"I'd like to take the dragon and wrap its tail around the base and give it some texture."

"I trust you, Erica, to do whatever you think will look good."

"I just need to photograph the bird. That's the only one I'm missing."

He raised his eyebrows. "I knew we'd get to this at some point." He took off his shirt to expose the small brown bird on his upper right chest.

"Not following," I said. "Its just a bird. Easy to do. It doesn't look that complicated. What kind of bird is it exactly?"

"It's a wren," he said.

"Why a wren?"

"Wren is my daughter."

I paused. I wasn't expecting him to have a child. "I'm sure she loves it." I snapped a few photos.

"I wouldn't know. She won't have anything to do with me. Can't say I blame her."

I set my camera on the worktable. "You two don't speak?"

"I never really knew her. I left her mother when she was a baby. Her mother and I were both kids. We were stupid and foolish, and I was real jerk back then. Oh, I was happy on the day Wren was born and I got this tattoo—it was my first one. But I just couldn't really handle it—being a father and all that, and her mother wanted us to get married. When the army came calling I left town so quick I never said goodbye."

"Ray, that's sad." I wanted to take notes, but I felt like this part of his life didn't belong on an index card.

"Is she who the urn is for?"

He nodded. "I'd hoped she and I might meet up before, well, you know." He shook his head.

"So," I was scrambling for words. "Who will the urn go to?"

He shrugged his shoulders. "I don't know now. I thought I'd

move forward and do it anyway. Maybe she'll change her mind. I didn't do anything for her growing up, but in case she wanted a part of me, you know, after it's all over, I wanted to know she had something she could touch, but I'm also hoping this is something she might want. It's me who wants to go home to her."

I put my hand on his arm and touched the tattoo.

"Sounds silly," he said. "I don't even know her."

My finger followed the outline of the bird like it was the borders of a map.

It seemed like from that day forward Ray was with me every day. I soon learned he had friends in town—other vets who all liked to do things like work on old motorcycles. Sometimes they rode back roads through the mountains together. I also learned that he and I had the same taste in music. We both loved classic rock, and he had old vinyl records and sometimes we'd just hang out and drink warm bourbon and play albums in their entirety. Sometimes he'd pop into the studio and bring me lunch or we'd grab coffee somewhere. Age and time started to blur, and it seemed like we hardly ever talked about anything heavy like cancelled engagements or dying. Just the opposite, we'd find ourselves laughing and making plans for the night ahead.

"Do you like to hike?" I asked him one day.

"It's okay," he said. "I'd rather ride Darla up on the Parkway." Darla was his vintage panhead Harley that he liked to spend time fixing up.

He conceded finally and joined me on a late fall hike.

"I want to get you up here before all the color is gone," I said, knowing this might just be the last weekend of color before it peaked and faded away.

We hiked through forested switchbacks that were the colors of green and brown grasses. We passed by gray rocks covered in spongy mosses. Mists faded in and out of the trail like they always do in the mountains regardless of the time of day. When we reached a lookout I found particularly pretty I held his hand as we walked toward the edge. Shades of red raged across the vista, swirling together like a cat's eye marble. Yellows and oranges that looked like a mellow mood on a summer day settled amongst the trees. Blues like sapphires dappled the branches. Purples, deep purples this year like I had not really ever seen, reminded me of the phlox that spring would bring. I looked at Ray and worried that maybe he wouldn't be here to see those phlox.

The evening started to set in as we lingered at first one vista and then another, taking our time. Winds picked up while the temperature dropped. We drew closer to each other and pulled out a blanket from his truck. He insisted we head back at one point. "It's crazy to be out here in this cold."

I didn't want to leave. I could see starlight and moonlight starting to glow. Nothing up here with Ray felt wasted. That night, on the mountain, I could see more black than gray in his hair. The lines around his eyes seemed to be shaded out by shadows from the moon. I recognized him as a young man. I could see what he looked like the night he came home from war, could see the man who loved a woman who gave birth to a girl named Wren and probably cried for months when she realized, like catching sight of a comet, that was the most she'd ever get of him.

Like a forest that grows back after a brush fire, he was taking something from all those ashes I was living in, but I was taking something too. His arms, his skin, his tattoos, his stories. None of him was wasted on me. He drew closer to me and we held each other, found each other, on the blanket through the night. The wind kept blowing in what felt like a circle all around us. I should have listened to him and left because it was cold and at times I was shivering. But I stayed. And so did he. Maybe he could be the potter for a while. Maybe I was the clay in all of this.

More than a year has passed since Ray died. He left me the name of a cousin who would handle delivering the urn to Wren. I like to imagine what her reaction might have been. I included all of my notes when I handed over the urn, hoping Wren would want them, would want to know stories about her father no matter how painful. I kept a small vile of his ashes for myself, and they sit on a ledge in my studio.

Today, it is the first Monday of spring. I walk into an art studio of a different sort. I've been talking off and on to an artist about what he is going to design for me. He shows me his final rendering.

As the artist's needle touches the inside of my wrist, and I am forever marked with ink and image, Ray's words linger. I finally know

COQUINA SOUP

We walk the beach like we always do when on the cusp of a big life change or decision. It's never intentional, this walk. The beach seems to appear like magic when we approach it and always on time, like the old friend who knows your story—your entire story and knows where and when you are drifting into delusion and doesn't have a problem reminding you that there might be another way of seeing the version you sell. The beach seems to know this, and without words it shuffles its riches onto the sand that is advertised to tourists as being white, but in reality it's the toasty brown of a biscuit top. The whitest sand goes to the highest bidders down the way with the fancy hotels. This stretch is not as known, and to me the sand under my feet feels more like grits and salt instead of cotton candy.

My mother was born on this beach. The daughter of Greek immigrants, they wanted each child to know the sea like kin. "We cut our baby teeth on seashells." She's told me the story so many times I feel like I, too, was birthed on this sand, but I wasn't. Yet, right as I was trying to figure out whether to go to college, or skip it and get a job, the ocean showed up. When my first boyfriend and I broke up the ocean showed up. When I had to decide to leave my job—one that I had poured all of my time and energies into despite the detriment to my marriage, the ocean showed up—this ocean.

And now, as I walk with my mother while a disease chips away at her body—and with my marriage coming to an end—this stretch of beach and water shows up like a carpet unfurling in front of me, and yet it feels like arms supporting us both from underneath, as if we are on top of it—floating on it's surface. Like it literally has our back.

"How is Ryan?" my mother finally asks.

"Good." I have not found the words to tell her that I have not seen Ryan in weeks, that we have lived apart for months. He was the "good one" my mother has always said. I was the benefactor of all the "luck of the stars" to have this one in my life.

"I used to do cartwheels on this beach," she tells me. Now, most of her time is spent in a wheelchair, but she finds the strength, with my help, to rise from it once every few days when I wheel her out to the shoreline so she "can just feel the sand under my feet."

"I don't think I can stay out here much longer," she says, but I want her to walk out deep enough so that the water can touch her knees. I want her to be able to reach the sandbar and dig her feet into the ocean's floor until her feet scratch up against the firm face of a sand dollar. But she cannot do any of this.

I look down and see the small thin outline of coquina shells pocked in the sand as the pull of the current draws some back and leaves others in clusters. Their pinkish pearlescent veneer sparkles when the sunlight hits their outer shells. We used to scoop these up with our hands, filling sherbet-colored plastic buckets to the brim.

I remind my mother of these memories, pointing down to the sand as the coquinas disappear.

"Coquina soup," she says and laughs. "We made it all the time."

My Greek grandmother, LuLu, my mother's mother, would collect these shells and scoop out the bits of meat inside and fill a large copper pot with a stock of water and salt, lemon and fish bones, and cook it down and then add the flecks of coquina meat. Her secret, she'd say, was a cup of chicken stock, not broth. She'd pour a stream of rich, thick, snowy-colored cream at the end and serve it to us piping hot with a sprinkle of Greek parsley on top that she clipped from a potted plant sunning on the porch.

"You'll live to be 100 if you eat this every day," she'd say as the bowls landed on the table, the soup vapors rising above them, clouding LuLu's image as she walked away.

Of course, she didn't make it every day. And she didn't live to be 100. But in my memories, she did.

My mother and LuLu, the family story goes, went back to Greece to get Cora, my great-grandmother—the family matriarch. She'd insisted on staying back in Greece, but as time wore her down, she agreed to finally make the journey to the states. How I envied that journey. I envisioned three generations of Greek women boarding a ship, setting sail for a once-in-a-lifetime journey. I would have loved to have been the fourth generation in that photo. Cora, LuLu, and my mother. And the coquina soup recipe that originated with Cora, and brought with LuLu from Greece, I imagined must have been tucked away in a box of recipes that would be passed on to the next generation yet to be born.

"We made the soup with what the sea washed up." My mother says this as she looks out onto the horizon, as if she is waiting for something, looking for something.

Washed up. What could be made with me? I wonder.

She turns her attention back to me. "You learn over time what to keep and what to toss back to the sea. Only you can know what is yours to keep."

Right now, I feel tossed back by Ryan. Yet I wanted him to want to keep me, to salvage me from the ocean, to see my worth as the most precious doubloons found in a buried treasure.

I reach down and scoop up a wet mushy ball of sand. It seeps through my fingers and back onto the beach. I have what appears to be a half-dozen coquinas in my grasp. They shimmy between my fingers trying to find their way back home.

"You should make it," she tells me. "You'll see it too. What to take, and what belongs to the sea." When I don't respond, she adds, "We came from Greek pirates, you know." She says this often when she doesn't know quite what to say.

This story has been told to me to many times. We were Greek pirates. Rebels. When our family came to Florida they weren't sponge divers, so our people didn't settle in the little enclave north of here, where all the sponge divers made their living by plunging into the brackish-colored waters pulling up the brown, rough and water-logged lumps that looked like meteors that had splashed into the sea. Our family traded on the elixir that is the child born of time and sugarcane. Our pirate ways, once again, had my family taking a path a little less crowded, a little more risky.

* * *

"Wheel me up to the edge of the window," my mother says after we are back inside the house. I put down the book I was reading and quickly move her.

"Look out there," she says. "One, two, three. Three catamarans!"

Like her, I count things I see out on the ocean—catamarans, windsurfers, cargo ships in the distance, low-flying planes pulling along advertising banners. I have been home now for three weeks, and this is the first time I have seen any catamarans.

"When Ryan gets here, you two should rent one."

Ryan won't be coming, and I've made the decision since arriving not to tell her about the divorce. It would be too painful for her. Her prognosis is a month at most. To look at her, though, at least a year is believable. I know that it could be a matter of days, weeks, and I'll soon call in help as she moves out of this world and into the next.

Ryan offered to come and see her. He always liked her. But I wanted these last few weeks with my mother to myself. It seems selfish now that I am here alone in her presence. My fingers flitter on the keypad on her house phone, always on the verge of dialing Ryan and telling him to just come on down. That vision is also laden with an image of our reconciliation. But I stop short because as much as I want him back, or think I want him back, I know he feels otherwise. I linger in these moments that are like my childhood with my mother when it was just our family—my mother, my father, now deceased, and myself.

"Any luck finding that last piece?" she asks. I wheel my mother into the main room where a puzzle of hot air balloons is in progress. When she last left off she was looking for the piece that had the edge of a daisy petal that would complete a field of flowers on the ground. She'd already assembled the balloon that floated in the air, but she couldn't find the piece that would finish the groundwork.

"No, Mama." I wheel her to the table. She puts on her readers and opens the pages to a magazine I have laid on table.

A knock comes at the door and I remember that Dr. Samuels is coming by to get Raisin, my mother's ailing dog. I have a hard time thinking of Charlie Samuels as the local vet, well, one of the local vets at least. Things have grown and changed since I returned. I can tell an old-timer from a newcomer based on which dry cleaner they frequent, what vet they use and if they love or hate Lamplight Pizza, which to a visitor is a dive, but to a local is the first food they crave if they've been away too long. I have memories of Charlie Samuels from high school hanging out there. He ran with the smart kids and so did I, just different ages, different grades. He and I always seemed to get along, but because of our age difference, we never became super close. My mom, because she was always enthralled with a pet—be it a cat or a dog—insisted on taking her pets to the senior Dr. Samuels and then when he passed on, the younger one.

I was happy to see Charlie when I opened the door, but when I turned around to see my mother's face, I noticed an enthusiasm in my mother I hadn't noticed before. I watched Charlie approach her. It was like she knew a Charlie I didn't know. He leaned down and hugged her, and it made me happy to see my mother so animated. I guess I'd been away longer than I thought. True, there were often long stretches between visits, but I could only surmise that in my mother's day-to-day all these years she and Charlie Samuels had seen more of each other than I realized.

"Hey there, Raisin." Charlie scooped her up and hugged her and then started checking out her eyes and mouth. Raisin had been sick several days. I was worried that her sluggishness indicated something serious. But with Charlie around, both Raisin and Mom found energy.

I let Charlie and Mom visit while I made tea. It was nice hearing them chatter in the other room and it was nice having a man around. My mind slipped briefly to Ryan, but as I lingered in the kitchen, I felt, for a moment, that having Charlie there, with mom and Raisin, was enough. Charlie was clearly at home, and this was even more evident when I heard Mother ask him to reach up to the top shelf and take down that blue-green glass jar. I remembered it was filled with coins and that Mom never let me touch it. She had another jar of coins she'd let me play with as a child. Coins that were just for me, all of them with my birth year that she had gathered for me when I was a baby, and those coins were easier for me to read because they were American quarters and nickels and pennies. She'd added to it here and there, and eventually the jar filled to the top. I called it my birthday jar, and I'd loved to empty all the coins onto the floor, spread them out and drop them back in.

When I bring the tea into the main room, Mom is explaining to Charlie that this jar was always very special because all the coins were from Greece.

She is happy to see him. Charlie Samuels was always a nice guy, attentive to old people at an age when kids had to be taught to be nice to old people. Being nice came easy to him.

Raisin runs to Charlie and jumps up on him. I like hearing my mother laugh with Charlie.

"Is Rebecca still all involved in her theatre work?" she asks him.

"Oh, yes," he says. "Her teachers are saying she might be a good candidate for a college scholarship."

My mother puts her hand on her chest. "That is wonderful, Charlie."

"Mama," I say, "you did a little acting in school, didn't you?" I place their water glasses on the table.

"Well, a little." She takes a sip. "But nothing like his Rebecca. She's going to be a star."

He turns his attention to me. "What about you, Sevesti? How have you been all these years?"

I don't know how to begin to answer his question, or how to end any answer I'd start. I shrug my shoulders, smile, stare out the window behind him, and begin counting the catamarans.

"I was thinking." He places his glass down on the table, ending the silence. "I'd like to take Raisin with me for a few days and run some tests on her. It would be easier on you both if I just handled getting her to the office and check her out there and then bring her back here."

I look over at my mother for her approval.

"If you think that would be best, I would appreciate that," Mom says, placing her hand over his. "You are a fine doctor." She smiles at him.

I remember my mother saying Charlie Samuels was the most handsome boy at my high school. And the most polite. She thought Charlie Samuels a "fine leader" and "gentleman." I wondered if somewhere deep inside she'd hoped I'd marry Charlie, but those are words she never expressed.

That night I put my mother to bed and I walk the beach. Ryan's face spins around in my mind. I want to tell my mother. I want her advice. I need my mother. But I can't lay all of this on her. I hate Ryan for his timing. I hate Ryan for his selfishness. I hate him for moving on without me. I hate him for backing out on a commitment that was supposed to be forever. I am ashamed to tell my mother that I made a desperate last-ditch effort to get him back—almost groveling. Shame wells up in me when I think about the scene I constructed. Summoning him to a sexy, couples-only hotel suite complete with candles, flowers and champagne. I provided all the carnal accouterments—lingerie and sex toys and even a video to ease any of his reluctance. But when he arrived, instead of a rekindled passion, I saw in his eyes pity and indifference. It was then that I realized I was competing with a phantom. Some woman—I think I called her a whore in our last argument—that I had no idea who she was, what she looked like, and worst of all, how she made him feel. It was something I used to know about him, like all those pathways on my palm that mother said were connected to the stars. Her unique way of reminding me that greater plans were always at work. I used to know these things. Now, I look down at the palms of my hands at all the lines that crisscross and converge; what I once saw as maps leading to endless discovery now look like boundaries.

I go back to the house and linger in the main room by lamplight. The windows in this room have never had coverings. The sea is always in view and even at night, although it's black outside, I can see the moonlight lightly brushing against the rolling sea.

I pace. I read. I look at the phone on the wall. I look at my phone to see if he has texted me. He has not. I pace some more.

I start to look at the things in her house. I rifle through drawers. I pull books off of shelves and look inside the pages to find old inscriptions that I hope are messages to me telling me what to do next.

I notice on the bookshelf the Mason jar of old coins, all from Greece. Once, when I was a child, I dumped the coins out and spread them across the floor to look at them—all foreign to me. My mother caught me with the coins and asked that I put them away and not touch them, She placed them high up on a shelf where I couldn't reach them, and I never dared to touch them again. But now as my mother sleeps, I reach for them—wanting to touch my childhood, wanting to re-connect with something that I know to be true.

Like I did as a kid, I open the jar and pour the coins all out onto the rug. I spread them out, and as I flip the coins over and examine them, the one thing that I notice again and again is the year. The coins are all from the same year, three years before my birth. Interesting. I place no real importance on it, though, until I turn the jar upside down. There is a piece of masking tape on the bottom. And what is written on the tape is a shock. What I read on the tape cuts through all of my emotions for Ryan and my marriage and my mother's imminent death. What I read calls into question everything I know about my mother, everything she has ever told me. What I read is proof that the old pirate ways never left our family. A name is scrawled in blue ink. It is a Greek name—Constantine, a name Americans often translated as Carl or Charles—or Charlie.

I am haunted by this revelation. I am overwhelmed, and yet at the same time, I am oddly soothed by this discovery. I realize that I in all the years I have known my mother, in all the years I have been her daughter, I thought I knew everything there was to know about her. And tonight, as I wrestle with keeping her safe from all of the drama in my life, I can only think about the drama my mother had to bury so many years ago. I want to wake her up and demand answers. Yet, the answers rush over me, and I need confirmation from no one. I want to make it right, and I want to soothe her. Part of me wants to rejoice and part of me knows it's not my place.

I do what I have always done, what my mother has always done. I walk out to the night ocean. I stand looking at a moon that is not full but more like a crescent. It looks as if it has tilted on it's side and spilled silver paint onto the tips of the cresting waves. If I was a kid, I'd take it as a sign that all the answers I am conjuring up in my mind are likely indeed true. But tonight, the truth is obvious and needs no celestial sign for confirmation: there never was a grand trip across the ocean to Greece to fetch my great-grandmother; it was a trip to take my pregnant mother to Greece to have her out-of-wedlock child. I can see vividly the old Olympic Airways bag hanging in my grandmother's closet. I flew once, never again. I recall hearing my grandmother saying these words as I boarded a plane for a school trip. It wasn't a ship that carried three generations of Greek women to America. That was a story of my own embellishing, I now realize. They came back—on a plane—a baby boy in tow. And if I really think back, I do remember hearing that Charlie Samuels was adopted. One of those facts I allowed myself to forget as kids often do, because why would I commit to memory something so random about a person? LuLu, I figured, likely wanted Mama to leave the baby in Greece, but knowing my mother, she must have protested. Bringing back Cora was a ploy. The baby, according to my weaving of these speculated facts, was given to the nice Dr. Samuels and his wife who could not have children. Charlie Samuels is an only child. And it was staring at me the whole time. Charlie's sunshine-y smile and dark thicket of espresso locks. He was Greek. He was my mother's child. And now I think of him caring for Raisin at this moment. Animals. My mother's ongoing commitment to having pets wasn't really about her love of dogs—it was a bridge to her son's life. It all made sense—old Dr. Samuels and his wife always had a fondness for my mother. They were always kind to her. And since I have been home paying her bills, and in all the years I reviewed her finances after my father died, I have never seen one payment to the veterinarian's office.

I continue to walk the dark beach at night with questions—who was Charlie's father? Certainly not my own. I knew the story of how my parents met—my father was in the military and deployed shortly after. No. It must have been a high school sweetheart. One she never spoke of in my presence. I thought about combing through the boxes in the attic and finding her yearbook. Certainly I could find some note scrawled in the pages or a heart drawn over his photo like schoolgirls often do. And what about Charlie? Did he know? My instincts told me no. It wouldn't have been done back then, not in a strict Greek family. That was the whole purpose of sending her off to Greece—to spare her the ridicule and shame that a teenage pregnancy from a fairly well-to-do family would invite. It was probably scandalous enough that my mother brought the baby back—a risky move on my mother's part, planting evidence right in the path of sunlight. But a risk she was willing to take, because if I know anything about my mother, she loves her family.

I figure no other Greeks know—just my mother's immediate relatives. I walk until I'm tired. Do I tell Charlie? Do I tell my mother about my divorce? Do I pull the jar of coins off the shelf and spill them onto the rug and tell my mother I know who these coins are meant for? I feel like I am on the loosing end of time. There are too many truths, and I am confused with where take the first step. My mother is dying.

These words swirl in my head. My mother is dying. This is the truth that ranks above all the others. What to do about it comes rushing at my feet as I look down at the water covering me up to my ankles, and before I can freeze this image in my mind, the water rushes back.

"You learn over time what to keep and what to toss back to the sea. Only you can know what is yours to keep."

I am up at sunrise the next morning. I go to the garage and take a bucket and small spade. I walk back out to the beach and spend the better part of an hour scooping up as many coquina shells as I can find. I remember my grandmother's instructions: "Scoop them up with your hands. When they see you coming, they try to run from you. But don't let that stop you. Keep scooping." I decide the spade is useless anyway. I place my hands in the sand, fingertips first, plunging into the cold grittiness that lies underneath the slick surface. I dig so deep that more water seeps up. Blindly I grab clumps and dump the mush I have collected into the bucket, sand and water and grit clinging to my fingers. I can faintly see little coquinas squirming around. The briny smell of seawater fills my bucket. I make several trips back and forth to the shoreline as I take each bucket load back up to the house and with a sieve rinse away the sand until I am left with a colander full of pink and gray and brown and orange shells shimmering in the sunlight.

I spend the morning trying to figure out how to open coquina shells. My mother is sleeping. I am in denial about how close it is to the end. But I am determined. I will do this one thing even though I am a notoriously terrible cook. I thumb through her recipe book and find an index card titled "Coquina Soup." The instructions are faded.

I boil the tiny shells until they pop open. I lay all of the shells out onto a towel I've spread across the kitchen table, and I pull and tug at the teeny bits of meat, rendering a paltry pile hardly enough to feed a cat. I return the spongy bits to the briny water and recall something about fish bones in broth, but it's not on the recipe card. My great-grandmother must have improvised this. I dig through the freezer and a bag of shrimp is as close as I get. I dump the bag into the water. While it boils, I refer back to the card and see I've skipped steps—sautéing onions, garlic, olive oil. I compensate random spices I find in the cabinet. I add olive oil, too. I am reminded, too late, that oil and water don't mix. I toss in the coquina and cover the pot.

I can remember LuLu sprinkling green flakes of parsley like fairy dust over each soup bowl. I look on the porch for a plant that looks like parsley. My family always called it "Greek parsley." I cannot recall any place outside of this beach town where I have ever heard of anyone use anything called "Greek parsley." But there are no potted plants anywhere. My mother lost interest in growing things when she got sick. I go back to the cabinet and find a jar of oregano and a jar of dill. It will have to do. When I lift the lid a confusing smell fills the air while bits of meat sadly bob around in a milky, spotted sea—like they are all drowning and have given up any hope of rescue.

I look at the clock. Charlie Samuels will be arriving to drop off Raisin. I cut a lemon and squeeze the juice into the pot. I toss in the rest of the lemon for luck. I cover the pot and let it simmer.

I break down and start to cry. I don't know the recipe. I never did. As the aroma of what I've prepared gets stronger, I am reminded of something Charlie and I indeed share: a version of our family history that isn't true.

When Charlie and Raisin arrive I have the table set for lunch, but I act like it's spontaneous.

"Charlie, stay and join us," I tell him. My mother is seated at the table, although in the few days since she has last seen Charlie and Raisin, she has declined. Charlie joins my mother and me, and we talk about his busy morning, his kids, animals.

"I made lunch," I say as I bring out the bowls of the soup on a tray and place one in front of my mother and another for Charlie and one for myself.

"Coquina soup," I tell Charlie. "It was a tradition made by my great-grandmother, my grandmother, and my mother."

"This must be a special soup."

"It is," I tell him. But I want to tell him more. I want to tell him everything. "It comes from Greece. From my great-grandmother."

"You mentioned that."

But I want to add, "Our great-grandmother."

Before he can swallow the first sip I find myself babbling.

"Do you like it? Is it hot enough? Too salty?"

He wipes his mouth with a napkin, a slight look of distaste on his face, but his politeness quickly shields it. "No. It's just fine. Delicious, in fact."

How I want him to have tasted the soup of our grandmother. How I wanted his bowl to have the right parsley, to have been prepared with coquinas that he would have, should have, scooped up with me as children. The bowl that sits before him, though, I feel is filled with lies.

"Mama," I say, "Do you like it?"

She nods. "Yes. It's wonderful, Sevesti."

"I've heard of coquina soup," Charlie says. "I don't think I have ever had it until now, though. My mother likes to make boring stuff like tomato aspic."

Aspic? I think about how his childhood is absent of all of the Greek traditions. Traditions my mother should have been able to show him. And now, here at the end, all he will ever know of her and our family is this bowl of questionable goo.

"Oh, yes," my mother chimes in. "Your mother makes a delicious aspic. She made it for a luncheon at the women's club years ago. Wonderful cook."

I think my mother must be lying, that she just wants to endear herself to Charlie. My mother has probably never had aspic in her life, but she would only want to say the nicest things about Charlie's mother, because she only wants Charlie to hear the nicest things. Much like my own childhood. She tells us what she wants us to believe to be true whether or not it actually is.

After lunch, Charlie helps me get my mother to her bed. Once she is asleep we walk back to the main room and Charlie confides in me.

"I didn't want to say this in front of your mother." He lowers his voice. "But Raisin is not well. She's very sick."

I nod. I have suspected this. Raisin has dropped weight. She hardly touches her food.

"I don't know how long she has," he adds. "But I'd like to be of help to you and your mom. I can take care of Raisin. My father thought the world of your mother, and I know if he were alive, he'd want to make things easy."

I put my hand on Charlie's arm and thank him.

Raisin runs up to Charlie as he turns to leave. He looks at the floor and notices something wedged up against the rug and reaches down to pick it up.

"Puzzle piece," he says, handing it to me.

I hold the missing piece in my hand.

"Raisin must have run off and hid it from us."

My mother passes within two weeks, passes not knowing that I know about her past, not knowing about my present. She passes believing Raisin is alive and happy. She passes without Charlie knowing the truth. All I have of this situation is my intuition, family stories, and speculation. I will pack up the house and her things. I will go back and face Ryan and the process of ending our marriage. I'll let the tide carry me for a while. I think about moving into this house with its creaky pine floors and endless windows to the sea. I wonder if I could live in the same town knowing Charlie Samuels and I share a secret he doesn't know. I wonder if I can be so much like my mother that the stories I weave overshadow the secrets I keep. I see Charlie once more before I leave.

"Mother wanted you to have this." I hand him the jar of Greek coins that I see as rightfully his. "The coins are from Greece. My mother brought them over with her when she was a teenager."

"Wow," he says. "Thank you, Sevesti. I'll cherish these." He holds the jar up to the light as if he is searching to see the faces on the coins and examine them further. It is my hope that I see this accurately.

He hugs me and turns to leave. But I want to grab him, hug him harder. I want to tell him all that I know. I want him to know that we are family.

"We come from Greek pirates!" I blurt out.

He turns and looks surprised and politely says, "You'll have to tell me about it someday."

But he doesn't realize that I mean him when I say we. And I hope for whatever "someday" means.

I watch him leave and wonder if he'll turn the jar over one day and read his Greek name, his original name, written on the bottom. I wonder if he will recognize what the shore has washed up for him . . . if he will know what to toss and what is his to keep.

RULES OF STARS AND ASH

Mama and I lived from location to location following an atlas of her failed relationships. Even though each new start might have only taken us to the other side of the county, to me if felt like it could be many cities away. Her moves were always sudden and her internal map was sketched by the repeated sweet talk coming from the same kind of man—rough, drunk, and womanizing. My mother had me young, a teenager herself, back when she caught the eyes of men, and in some ways that attention became her addiction. I had no choice but to follow along on her ride on a map that seemed to have no real destination. And the thing about maps is that they never go in a straight line.

A constant throughout this was a man I knew as Ralph. He would show up here and there to help nurse my mother through the latest broken heart. Sometimes he'd bring Mama a six-pack of beer or a bottle of cheap wine. He managed cattle and horses and was always in and out of work. He smelled of wet hay and animal sweat. He existed on drinking binges and frequent forays with random women. One or the other usually the cause of his shoddy work record.

On the heels of my mother's latest break-up—we'd been living over an auto repair shop with Jake, a mechanic my mother was seeing until he skipped town, leaving her with no place to live—Ralph showed up to save the day and knew of a situation for us where we could live in the stable hands' quarters on the property of a rich lady on the outskirts of town. He was leasing some of her land for his cattle. We'd heard a few whispers about this lady, partly because her faith was in question by the locals. They were suspicious of her private ways. Some even suggested she practiced witchcraft.

My mother acted like it was a failure to have to turn to this woman for work. But I was intrigued. All we had to do was go meet her and see if she liked my mother well enough to bring her on as her personal caregiver. Ralph looked over at me. "There might be even be some housework for you, Chevy. "

Mama arranged some borrowed clothes for me from a family at her church. Walking up the brick path that led to Mrs. Phoebe Magnus' large home—big columns, wide front porch, and large double front doors with a large brass doorknocker—my mother straightened my collar and pushed my walnut colored braids off my shoulders.

"Chevy, don't mess this up for me," she ordered. This, I was used to: remaining obedient in the face of whatever Mama was trying to make happen for herself. Usually it involved me not getting in the way of the men in her life. And now it was her getting a job.

"What will I be doing here?" I asked, wanting to know how my young life would change. I was only fourteen, but I had friends and school and wasn't entirely uninterested in fun.

"Whatever she asks," she said.

A petite woman wearing a head wrap of multi-colored metallic fabric greeted us. Her name was Bijou. She was Haitian and her accent sounded like music to me. Bijou was the current caregiver. The "heavy stuff," like helping Mrs. Magnus in and out of bed, was taking a toll on her back, and she was ready to train someone for her job. My mother worked in a bar three nights a week and that job she could keep. Bijou reached her hand out to me. "Looks just like you," she said and smiled at my mother. I could sense my mother's annoyance with this statement—just like you, but younger. I was walking evidence of her mistakes and her loss of freedom.

Bijou escorted us into a grand foyer, and I wasn't prepared for the startling decor. The interior of the house was like a kaleidoscopic portal to the world. It overwhelmed me in a way I had never known. Colors and textures and the spirit, the essence, of all the pictures I had seen in geography and history books at school all melded into exposition on the walls and surfaces of her home—the curated result of a lifetime of Mrs. Phoebe Magnus' travels. Rugs from India lay on wood floors as if announcing refinement's sovereignty over the house. Multi-colored lamps from Morocco hung throughout the house. Paintings depicting all sorts of places and people (some of the people looking distorted) were framed in gilded gold, and there seemed to be no room in the house not covered in art. I noticed all the ceilings of the house were different painted versions of the night skies. I would come to learn over the new few weeks about the house from Bijou as she trained my mother and, at times, me. I would come to learn about Mrs. Magnus, though, on my own.

"Bijou." The voice commandeered the living room. And it was then that I first saw Mrs. Magnus. She was a long form of a woman who appeared quite tall, even though she was in a wheelchair. She was lean, her face bearing angular, high cheekbones of an established and curated lineage, and she was wearing an emerald green robe that had the appearance of a fancy gown. She wore her black hair in a large bun on top of her head. The gaze of her deep charcoal eyes locked in on me. Then she looked us both up and down, my mother and I, gave a wave of her hand to Bijou, as if saying, "I'm not impressed, but they'll do," and wheeled herself out of the room.

And like magic, my mother and I were living on the property in a two-room, cinderblock structure that had space only for a sink and a rusty refrigerator that smelled of stale beer when opened and some recliner that was left behind by the last stable boy. A crude toilet covered in peach rust stains stood exposed in what was the bedroom that had a twin bed pushed against the wall.

I went about my business going to school. I was an average student. I struggled and had little direction. At night, I'd sometimes lay a blanket on the grass outside the stable quarters and look up at the dappled starlight that washed over the hill where Phoebe Magnus' house stood. To me, the house looked like what wholeness must be—life's success displayed in the abundance of tangible things. I would come to learn that those stars dangling over her land like a mobile in the sky were more to Phoebe Magnus than flecks of celestial light. To her, they were like lyrics—incantations that ordered her days.

My duties in the house were small things I could do after school. I polished silver, ironed linens, dusted shelves. One chore which I thought odd was making sure Phoebe's candles were extinguished after supper. Phoebe had lots of peculiarities and quirks, and one of them was her obsession with candles and incense. Candles were lit even in glaring daylight. And she insisted on incense. Not every day, but often enough. The scent bothered my mother, but I loved it instantly and felt transported when the aroma of vague cold smoke and crisp wood filled the house. Ash from the incense would sometimes spill onto the floor and I would pretend to see shapes or patterns to how they fell on the floor and imagine them to tell a story. I was dutiful and responsible, and under my watch, the candles were extinguished nightly; but secretly, it made me sad as I wanted the flames and incense smoke to carry me into the night.

It was at night, when Phoebe went to bed, that I would come to life. I felt a freedom to roam around the house and no rush to return to the stable quarters. A room of great interest to me was Phoebe's library. It housed not only shelves and shelves of books that I became lost in, but it also was the landing spot of her collection of exotic relics and taxidermy. It was this room that probably gave shape to the rumor that shadowed Phoebe: that she practiced the ways of the occult. I found several volumes of books about astrology, tarot, and horoscopes on her shelf, and I felt oddly at home amongst the stuffed owl, the pheasant and the antlers that were hung on the wall. One night, I crossed paths with Mrs. Magnus in the library, and it made me nervous, like I was rifling through her things. She'd caught me gazing at a row of masks she had hanging on the wall. They were tribal and frightened my mother (she called them "not of God"), but not me.

"You like those?" Mrs. Magnus' voice came from the entry of the library.

I nodded. "I think they're interesting." I didn't have quite the words to express what I felt inside about them. To look at them made me feel like I was touching a spot on the earth I had never been to nor had even imagined.

"They came home with me when I was probably about your age," she said, pointing at them. "They're from west Africa. Have you ever traveled, Chevy?"

I shook my head. I'd never even been outside of our county.

"Well, then." She wheeled herself to one of the bookshelves and pulled a few titles. "Good thing we have a library. We'll start with these."

She handed me a stack of books by people I had never heard of before—Jane Austen, Emily Dickinson, George Orwell, Charles Darwin, Khalil Gibran, Anne Frank, F. Scott Fitzgerald. I read a book by someone named Nietzsche and another by a man from Russia with the name Nabokov. I read Madeleine L'Engle, C.S. Lewis, H.G. Wells, and Arthur C. Clarke. She introduced me to Henry Miller and Allen Ginsberg. I can't say I understood all of these books. But that didn't seem to matter to me. What I didn't understand stood like a placeholder for me—something I knew I'd get back to later. I couldn't get enough of those books.

"Read these, and others, as you please," she said. "You need not ask my permission."

I thanked her, holding the old books in my hand. Over the next few nights, down in the stable house, I got lost in chapter after chapter. My mind was opening up to people in a way I had never been exposed to before—people who spoke differently, dressed differently and believed in things I had never heard of before. For me, every book was like getting to travel on a plane to a new place..

Soon, I found myself looking forward to those evenings when my mother was working in the bar and I could linger up at the Magnus house longer than usual. I came to crave her library and I didn't know why. And Phoebe would meet up with me more and more in that room full of shelves. As the months progressed, we'd talk about books and science, and stars and travel. Sometimes I'd make her tea and she'd say I should drink tea as well. Her tea was different, she told me. It was cardamom, and it was common in India—and she stored it in a spice box from Zanzibar. All the things she told me were like an intoxicating secret that no one else in our little town would ever know or understand.

When I left her house on those nights, I'd walk down through the pasture that separated our spaces feeling so grown up and smart. It was new to me to feel like I might know things, think things. I wondered what my mother would think of my ideas, and of me. I laughed, picturing her saying, "It's not of God," as if holding up a gold shield or cloaking herself in chainmail. It's not as if my mother attended church every Sunday and was piously devout, but the books and items I found interesting clearly bothered her.

On some of those nights after I left Phoebe's house, I'd be alone down at the stable house while my mother's shift at the bar still had hours to go, and Ralph's truck would pull up to the door.

"Your mama around?" he'd ask. When it was clear she wasn't, he'd linger a while talking to me, asking how school was. He'd wait until my mother got home, and while they spent time making out and eventually going into the bedroom and closing the door, I'd find myself alone with no one to talk to and nowhere to go. Often, I'd go outside and throw down a blanket on the grass and stare up at the sky. Eventually I'd wander back into the house and drift off to sleep on the couch, and sometimes the closing of the door after Ralph would leave is what woke me up and became a kind of alarm clock for me to get up and get ready for school

One night, during one of Ralph's visits, while he and my mother were back in her room, I went outside once again, to lay a blanket on the grass and stargaze. But on this night, as I looked up at the Magnus House, I swear I could see a dim light in the corner room that I knew was Phoebe Magnus' bedroom. It would be odd for her to be awake at this time of night. Even though it was so far away, I believe I could see her in the window

The next day, Mrs. Magnus, without explanation, ordered my mother and me out of the stable house and into the main house. And without explanation, Mrs. Magnus terminated Ralph's lease on the land and his cattle were removed.

My mother did not like the new living arrangement at all, but I relished it. Bijou was already gone and my mother was able to take on the role of night nurse, although reluctantly. Mrs. Magnus increased my mother's pay so she would no longer need to keep working at the bar. Although I was happy to see mother gain a more stable job, I missed the time I had alone in the house, especially in the library where I could let my curiosities wander and could flip through the pages of the most questionable books. I missed the time I'd spent with Mrs. Magnus alone where I could broach topics off limits to my mother, even topics that I now know were political or spiritual questions; these were not the types of conversations I would have had with my mother. My mother's world was one centered around her town, or "my kind" as she liked to say. She said it was bad to be a "curious, thinky" type, that those girls were just "no fun" and would end up "all alone." She discouraged me spending so much time in the library and wished I would "go put on some lipstick." She didn't want me reading books, but would sometimes bring home copies of magazines with glossy covers and articles with titles like "How to know what he is thinking without him knowing you know." I'd flip through them, of course; and some of the photos I tried to copy in terms of making myself look older. But I would still feel that pull of the library and all those books covered in leather or cloth. The relics on the shelves covered in glass cloches, like bird nests from nature hikes, or bones from an archaeological dig, all called to me. I loved the sense of discovery as Mrs. Magnus showed me the collections from her travels: the lip plate from southern Ethiopia; the fez she brought back from something she called the "Grand Bazaar" in Istanbul or the silk Thangka painting from Tibet. The Thangka painting was religious, and I knew my mother would disapprove because it wasn't "of God."

But to Mrs. Magnus, all of these things were indeed "of God." Even her books about the stars—especially constellations. She loved to talk about how life on earth corresponded with the stars. I didn't really understand what she was saying, but that didn't bother me because listening to how she saw the world was like permission to dream. And I wasn't used to dreaming.

As I got older, living in that castle of a house, I started to find more autonomy. I spent my sixteenth birthday there and was even allowed to invite a few friends over for a cake. I started to feel as if I owned the house at times, as my chores seemed to diminish in favor of "time to study" as Mrs. Magnus directed, while my mother's duties increased. Friends started to come home with me after school, and we'd watch a movie or play a game of snooker in the game room. My grades at school started to improve as Phoebe insisted I have a tutor, and she paid for one to come to the house twice a week to help me improve my grades before graduation.

Mrs. Magnus sat me down one day after my tutor left. "You need to start applying to schools, Chevy. I've even taken it upon myself to do some research for you."

I was intrigued. College? For me? College sounded like another planet. I couldn't imagine how I would get there. I couldn't imagine what it was all about.

"You can use my address as yours," she said. "You should apply to the state university. It's only three hours north of here, and I'll help you with the tuition."

I was so young, that now, when I look back, I clearly didn't understand the weight of it all.

"I have no children of my own," she said. "And I've got a legacy that should be passed on to someone. I have great faith you will succeed at college."

"How will I even get there?" I said.

"You found your way here, did you not?"

"But I am here only because of my mother."

"Are you, though? You could have not come with your mother that first day. You could have not stayed. You could have packed your bags and run away during the night. Who is to say you did not choose to be here, Chevy?"

I suddenly saw university as my choice. In that second, things that were once dream-like began to feel like things I could touch.

My mother, however, was becoming increasingly unhappy with how things were evolving. She felt confined to the house of a suspected atheist, at best, and someone who practiced the occult at worst. I heard her say to a friend, *"She doesn't believe in God, and she thinks she owns me and is filling my girl with all kinds of hooey! Making her think she's gonna go off to New York or Paris, France or something. First chance I get, I'm gettin' us out of here."*

To offset what I would hear and learn in the library, my mother began to attend church much more often and insisted I attend with her. Her church met on a weeknight in an old warehouse. I'd go with her and sit beside her as she smugly smiled to the preacher. I suspected he had a thing for my mom, even though he was married. He knew my mother from high school and was always "needing to have a quick word with her" after church let out. I sometimes even wondered if he was the real reason we began attending more often in the first place.

I sat there though and listened to sermon after sermon about a savior that we had all assembled here to love and know and find. I listened to how incomplete I was, as we all were, until we found this savior. The words, however, never seeped into me, but they did seem to do so to the others seated around me. I watched them raising their arms up in song and swaying in unison to music being played from a band up on a stage. Her church felt like a rock concert and less like the traditional quiet churches I'd attended with friends at school when I had a sleepover at their houses. At those churches, people were reserved and staid, there was an altar, and I recognized other kids from school and felt oddly at home in their churches. But at my mother's church, I noticed only a few girls my age, yet none of them were from my high school because at this church schools were considered something to be suspicious of, and these kids were all taught at home. I wondered what these people would think about Mrs. Phoebe Magnus and her candles and taxidermy and books about Voodoo and tarot. What would they think about the prayer flags she had from Tibet or the spears that hung on the wall from the Masai tribe in Africa or the touristy clock she brought back from Turkey that chimed the Muslim call to prayer.

One girl I did recognize, though. I knew her from school, though I didn't know her very well. I remembered she'd dropped out because she got pregnant. I now saw her sitting with a baby on her lap. My mother looked over at her smiling.

"Don't you know her from school, Chevy?" she said. "You should give her a call. It'd be good for you to hang out with some girls from church. What a cute baby, too."

I continued to watch the people sway and sing and I tried hard to follow suit. But it felt forced and the spark just never struck me.

Some people would fall to their knees, tears bleeding down their faces, and their voices would start to roll and roll in words undecipherable. I felt my mother touch my arm once when this happened.

"One day," she said and nodded and smiled at me, "it will happen for you, too. Don't you worry. I know it." Though I noticed it had not happened to her. And I hoped that what I was watching would never, ever happen to me.

One morning, I woke to a startling argument happening in the house. I jumped from my bed and walked down the hall and through the main living area, and from the kitchen I could hear very clearly the voices of my mother and Mrs. Magnus.

"She is my daughter," I heard my mother say. "You have filled her with enough of these damn lies."

"But going to college is not filling her head with lies, Nadine," Mrs. Magnus said. "I'm just trying to help her have more opportunities."

"Opportunities for what?" my mother answered.

"A life outside of this little town. There is nothing here for her. She is going to graduate soon, and it's just something I want to offer to her."

"You'll do no such thing. My daughter has no interest in your fancy university filled with a bunch of—"

And it was there that my mother stopped short, but I knew what she was going to say. She was gong to call them all heathens, or gypsies or some other sort of slur. I knew that even not saying the words had already crossed a line with Mrs. Magnus. I started to panic. I wanted to jump in the middle of it and stop it. I wanted my mother to stop it.

Apparently, Mrs. Magnus had announced to my mother she would pay for me to go to college. Suddenly I was nervous. It was like time had caught me, and Mrs. Magnus was correct. I would be graduating in a year. I had no ideas for the future. In that split second, I felt like I was indeed on my mother's path and not my own. I tiptoed back to my bed because I could feel that a change had just transpired and I needed to be ready.

Within a week, my mother came bursting into my room after school with "good news." She started pulling my clothes out of the drawers and closets.

"We need to get packing," she said. She was beaming with happiness. She moved in a flurry. "No more of this haunted place. We have a new start, a new home, and we'll all be a family." I was disoriented, not sure what was happening.

"We're moving again?" I said.

"Yes, Chevy," she said, still rummaging through drawers. "I snagged me a good one. Finally woke up and got my senses about me. You and me and Ralph! Me and Ralph are gonna get us a place. We'll be family. The three of us."

I was shocked. Frozen.

"You should probably start calling him Daddy, now that we're gonna be living together. I knew that Phoebe Magnus was a loon when she run him off the property. Well, we'll show her. We will. Who's having the last laugh now?" She grabbed my hands and clutched them tight.

"Chevy, this is like a dream come true. I am finally getting it right. I've picked the right man. He was here all along. And guess what?"

I was speechless.

"He is so excited to be a daddy to you. He said he's missed having you around, and you was always like his own daughter."

In that moment, I forgot to breathe.

She stuffed all my clothes into a garbage bag, did the same with hers, and threw our things into the car. Like that, we were gone. I never got to say goodbye to Phoebe. Another journey on my mother's atlas had come to an end.

Ralph found his way to living in a decrepit banged-up trailer on the other side of the county and my mom and I moved in. I followed my mother's instructions to get better at domestic chores—cleaning, sewing, ironing. Later I heard, through a girl at school whose mother became Mrs. Magnus' night nurse, that she was slipping in health. A stroke finally took what was left of her mobility as well as her voice. I wondered if this girl now spent her nights in the library amongst the owls and pheasants and bones and books.

As graduation approached, I decided to make an unannounced visit to see Mrs. Magnus. When I arrived, my mother's replacement answered the door. Her name was Valerie, and she said Mrs. Magnus couldn't take any visitors because she was too ill. I didn't want to make a bother of myself, so I complied and turned to go quietly, but Valerie stopped me and said that there was a piece of mail that had arrived a week earlier. She said she didn't have a forwarding address for me. I took the envelope, saw it was from a college, and went home, too afraid, somehow, to open it.

That night, I took a blanket outside and laid it on the ground. Looking up at the night sky, I picked out Andromeda and Pisces, which I could now name. I knew that there would be nights ahead that I'd spot constellations not seen from where I lay now. I wondered if, even as Phoebe lay ill, someone in that house knew to light her candles and incense. I wondered, if like me, the new girl in the house wanted the scent of the incense to linger; if she was sad to extinguish the candles.

All the constellations in the night sky seemed to ripple in a haze. I laid back onto the blanket and closed my eyes, pretending I could hear waves crashing and could smell salt in the air. I held the envelope and opened it against the starlight. Every constellation, every dot of light, looked like a potential path to choose. I opened the letter with a return address from the university where Phoebe had mailed my application. I held the page up, trying to illuminate the words. I had been accepted. I could make out the start date of the approaching semester. It was just a few months away. I could work odd jobs. I could try to save. I could find a ride.

On the back of the envelope I noticed Phoebe Magnus's handwriting. She had scrawled the words "I will help."

It was like the sky had selected me for baptism. I decided then to choose the path lined with things that aren't things, but rather formed with what cannot be taken.

Although I could see starlight raining down all around me, I knew, in that moment, it was actually me emitting the luster.

ACKNOWLEDGMENTS

The earlier versions of the below stories have been featured in the listed outlets:

- "Empty Places" appears in the *The New Guard Literary Journal* Spring 2021 and was a finalist in the Machiogionne Fiction Contest
- "Honeycomb" appears in the *Broadkill Review*, 2022
- "Mangroves" appears in *Quail Bell Magazine*, 2022
- "Coquina Soup" appears in *VIA: Voices in Italian Americana*, Spring 2023

Thank you to my editor, Nicholas Grosso for your time, patience, and belief in my writing.

ABOUT THE AUTHOR

A fifth-generation Floridian, FRANCES NEVILL writes fiction and non-fiction deeply influenced by the landscape and history of her home state. She earned her undergraduate degree from Florida State University and completed her Master of Fine Arts in Creative Writing from Converse University. This is her debut short story collection.

VIA Folios

A refereed book series dedicated to the culture of Italians and Italian Americans.

www.ingramcontent.com/pod-product-compliance
Lightning Source LLC
Chambersburg PA
CBHW020025030726
47499CB00007B/2281